THE LOW ROAD

THE LOW ROAD

Reginald Hill

This title first published in Great Britain 1998 by
SEVERN HOUSE PUBLISHERS LTD of
9–15 High Street, Sutton, Surrey SM1 1DF.
Originally published in 1974 under the title
Death Takes the Low Road
and pseudonym of *Patrick Ruell.*
This title first published in the U.S.A. 1998 by
SEVERN HOUSE PUBLISHERS INC of
595 Madison Avenue, New York, N.Y. 10022.

British Library Cataloguing in Publication Data

Hill, Reginald, 1936-

   The Low Road
   1.   Highlands (Scotland) - Fiction
   2.   Thrillers
   I.   Title
   II.   Ruell, Patrick, 1936- . Death takes the low road.
   823.9'14 [F]

   ISBN 0 7278 5335 X

Typeset by Hewer Text Composition Services Limited,
Edinburgh, Scotland.
Printed and bound in Great Britain by
MPG Books Ltd, Bodmin, Cornwall.

For Milly

Oh you'll tak the high road
And I'll tak the low road
And I'll be in Scotland afore ye.
For me and my true love
Will never meet again...

Loch Lomond

I

It was a Tom and Jerry day. Clarity had gone beyond perspective. The mountains lay flat against the sky and their precise image hung bat-like in the unflawed mirror of Loch Coruisk. Colours were primary. The blues of sea and loch, the green of the grass, the brown of earth and stone, all had flowed direct from an MGM cartoonist's brush.

Hazlitt lay in his sun-warmed saucer of rock and felt content to be two-dimensional. In two dimensions trouble could just come from the sides and nothing was going to come at him over the Cuillins to the west or the Red Hills to the east. The beauty of Skye in any mood was a blessing. Today it was an earnest of divine benevolence and bliss eternal.

Perhaps it's going to be all right, mused Hazlitt. Perhaps they're all just going to forget about me, and after a couple of weeks I'll go back to the university and sit in my office and do my job and no one will even mention that I've been away.

He rolled over like a fat cat in the sun. It was a good image. A marmalade cat, with his gingery hair, thinning a little as he reached towards forty but with the present compensation of a golden stubble on lip and chin. A disguise? Hardly. Shaving was too tedious when you lived in a tent, that was all.

So. A marmalade cat. Short; a bit paunchy despite the Wednesday-night squash and the Sunday-morning twenty lengths of the swimming pool; lacking a cat's lithe grace of movement, except in the water, but with all its easy indolence, its built-in hedonism, its instinct for survival. Especially the instinct for survival.

A bead of sweat trickled off his forehead and smeared the left lens of his large round spectacles. It was even warmer than he had thought. He rubbed the glass clean with a khaki handkerchief and looked back longingly to the still, dark waters of the loch. But it would be a couple of hours before he could slide gratefully into its depths. A pair of cormorants winged silently a foot above the surface. Strange sinister birds: he could never recall seeing them rise any higher into the air.

He turned now and looked out to sea. Absolute calm. Blue modulated into green and all into the eerie nothing of a heat mist an immeasurable distance from the shore. Fifty yards? A mile? It didn't matter. Today was a Tom and Jerry day. Distance did not exist.

It was getting late. Perhaps something had happened. Perhaps the boat wouldn't come today. His heart leapt at the thought. Perhaps he could rise now and descend to the loch, wash the heat from his body, then return to his well-concealed tent and grow warm again.

The distant putter of an outboard motor disposed of the dream before it could take a hold. With a sigh he reached for his binoculars and scanned the sea for a glimpse of the boat which twice a day in good weather re-created the unwanted third dimension.

Now he saw it. Out of the heat mist it came, low in the water. No wonder it had been late; it was packed to capacity.

Carefully he scanned the passengers through the small battlements of loose rock he had built to protect himself as much as possible from a return scrutiny. The usual

8

lot. Family groups mainly; he tried to read their backgrounds in their faces. An old couple. Retired businessman, perhaps. A younger couple in their thirties. Most of the five kids on the boat seemed to be theirs. Two middle-aged women. Schoolteachers, he felt sure. Had been taking their hols together for thirty years. Another young couple, gay in matching tartan shirts. Very affectionate. Honeymooners?

He felt lonely. They always made him feel lonely. Paradoxically, left to himself he never experienced loneliness.

But they were transient, ephemeral, unreal creatures. Here for an hour, then gone, leaving the fat marmalade cat to soak up his unique sun. He smiled at the thought, still moving slowly down the boat with his glasses. Then he stopped smiling.

Sitting in the thwarts next to the familiar figure of the weather-gnarled, whisky-cured old boatman was a man. He clearly did not belong with any of the family groups. Burly, impassive, he wore a light fawn raincoat and dark brown trilby despite the heat of the day. In his hands he held a pair of field glasses which he now raised and focussed on the shore.

His heart racing, Hazlitt slipped back into his saucer of rock. Even at this distance there was no doubt in his mind. He felt panic clawing at his guts.

It was still a Tom and Jerry day. But the colours and the heat and the light had helped him to forget for a few foolish moments that his was not the role of the cat basking in the sun.

He was Jerry, the mouse, and out there approaching nearer with every moment was the implacable hunter, Tom.

'I really can't see what all the fuss is about,' said the grey man mildly.

9

'He's a menace. He has to be stopped,' answered the young man.

'He's just frightened, that's all. Many "sleepers" react like this when you try to wake them. It's been nearly twenty years.'

'Twenty years of indulgence, materialism, hedonism. You should have spotted the signs.'

'They were part of the cover,' said the grey man shaking his head at his companion's naivety. 'What did you want him to do? Go around with a big banner saying *I, William Blake Hazlitt, am still a good party member, despite all appearances to the contrary?*'

The young man shook his head at this unbecoming levity.

'Control is very angry,' he said.

The grey man shrugged indifferently.

'Control is two thousand miles away,' he said. 'And it was Control's idea to wake Hazlitt with this assignment. For God's sake, what did they expect? After all these years as a university administrator, he's supposed to become James Bond overnight?'

'He was the man for the job.'

'Which he may yet perform. Give him time to think and he'll come back ready to co-operate fully.'

'You think so?' The young man was openly scornful. 'Meanwhile we do nothing, is that your answer? And if British Security get hold of him, what then?'

'He'll say nothing,' said the grey man.

'No. I'll see to that.'

The young man nodded vigorously as he spoke.

The grey man mustered all the authority at his disposal and said sternly:

'You will not forget to check with me before initiating any action.'

The young man laughed.

'My men have been at work for days now. I am expecting results very shortly. My kind of action rarely permits time for any checking.'

He left the room without a farewell. The grey man stared blankly at the open door. The young man had finally stepped into the open and challenged him. He should have foreseen it. His masters were extremely unsentimental men and whoever resolved this present situation with maximum dispatch and minimum fuss would receive their approval. The grey man had little doubt that his appraisal of the situation was correct. Left alone or even chivvied along a little, Hazlitt would return. But theories were no good unless proved. And the young man's solution would pre-empt proof.

He reached for the telephone. What little positive action he could take, he would take. But for the moment all he could hope for was that Hazlitt had some hidden talent for survival.

Hazlitt scrambled recklessly down the rock slope towards the loch. The sweat on his face was no longer just the result of the sun.

In the still air he could clearly hear the stutter of the outboard motor as the boat pulled away from the shore. Where it went now he was uncertain. To drop or check on the boatman's lobster pots, probably. But in an hour it would return to pick up the tourists and take them back to Elgol, delighted to have penetrated to regions untrodden by man—or at least by more than a few thousand trippers every summer.

The attraction of Loch Coruisk, apart from the natural beauty of the setting, was its inaccessibility by land. No roads came anywhere near. The mountains rose protectively on all sides except the seaward. Only the enthusiastic and experienced walker—or a man driven by a desperate need for seclusion—would make his way there on foot, following the turns of Glen Sligachan for many miles before taking to the high ground and laboriously climbing more than two thousand feet. Hazlitt remembered his sense of triumph and achievement when at last, stout Cortes-like, he had gazed down on the dark-shining length of the hidden loch.

At the moment only the stoutness remained. He had begun to feel quite fit after these few days of life in the open, but suddenly he was puffing like a donkey-engine as he trotted along the edge of the loch towards his tent, concealed in a fold of ground a couple of furlongs away.

Logic told him it was far from certain the man in the fawn raincoat was a Tom. Over the past few days he had convinced himself that (a) he wasn't important enough to he searched for and (b) he had covered his tracks so well that he was unfindable anyway. The daily routine of watching the trippers arrive was merely a time-filler. They would clamber over the rocky shelf from the sea until the loch came in view. Even those energetic enough to want to go further hardly had the time.

So why was he risking a cracked ankle or worse by rushing madly over this dangerous terrain? At the very worst Tom would just be investigating a report that a lone man was camping by Loch Coruisk.

Though if that was worth investigation they must have followed his laboriously concealed trail to Skye.

The thought made him accelerate and he did not slow down until he reached his tent. It was well situated from a camper's as well as a fugitive's view. He had always been a keen explorer of the Great Outdoors. But over the years his equally keen exploration of the Great Indoors had worked insidiously on his frame of mind and body, and since the age of thirty he had set up his base camps under hotel roofs, not canvas. But the gear had remained and the expertise was slowly returning.

Expertise was one thing, common sense was another, he thought, as he squatted down by the tent. He should have remained in his observation saucer, taken note of fawn-coated Tom's activities, watched him safely on to the boat. If anything *had* been spotted and remarked on by a party of climbers, say, or some native of the hills, it was likely to be his tent. Even a rough positioning would dramatically cut the odds against a searcher finding it in an hour.

No. *Half* an hour. He would have to leave time to get back and be picked up by the boat. He glanced at his watch. Amazingly twenty-five minutes had already passed since he saw the boat arrive.

He felt reassured, but it was better to be safe. With a sigh he rose to his feet again and moved off uphill to the right. He knew the terrain well and now he was no longer in a panic, he moved with sure-footed ease till he reached his secondary observation point. He lay down in the heather and carefully wormed his way forward to the skyline. From here it was impossible to see the boat, but he had an excellent view of the rocky ridge which separated the loch from the sea and which was as far as most of the trippers penetrated.

Slowly he brought up the glasses. Most of those from the boat were visible. The children seemed to be enjoying their adventure. The girl in the tartan shirt sat talking to the old couple. She pointed upwards, probably to where her new husband had scrambled in an excess of virility. Hazlitt moved his glasses in search of him but stopped as different and more rewarding prey was trapped by the lens.

Tom, ludicrous in his raincoat and hat, was sitting uncomfortably on a boulder, making what seemed like a systematic sweep round the loch through his field glasses. When they swivelled in his direction Hazlitt buried his face in the heather and counted slowly to a hundred before looking once more.

In the next fifteen minutes the routine was repeated

four times. Then, blessedly, one of the children spotted the returning boat and at their differing speeds they all moved out of sight down the seaward side of the ridge.

Tom was last to go. He stood up slowly, as though his muscles had stiffened, half-turned, then unexpectedly brought the glasses up once again and for a split second seemed to focus directly on Hazlitt's hiding place.

Hazlitt pressed his face so violently into the heather that his nose struck rock and the bridge was grazed. When he looked again it was a soothing sight to see Tom's head and shoulders outlined momentarily against the royal blue sky before he too dropped out of view towards the sea and the boat.

Hazlitt gave it another ten minutes till the stuttering of the motor had faded completely away.

He rolled over on his back and smiled at the sky. Perhaps his instinct had been wrong. Perhaps there had been no danger.

No. The road of complacency was the road to disaster. He would have to make plans to move. But not just now. Loch Coruisk was his until the afternoon boat brought another pack of tourists. He rose and made his way in pleasurable anticipation down past his tent to the water's edge. The sun was at its zenith. It was gloriously hot, had been hot ever since he arrived. From his previous experience of Skye, he knew such weather was almost unprecedented. It certainly couldn't last, but while it did . . .

Quickly he stripped off. The first time he had braved the chilly waters he had with absurd coyness changed behind a towel into his swimming shorts. But now his buttocks, though still paler than his legs and torso, were no longer the absurd pink outcrops they had been.

Carefully he placed his spectacles in his left boot. Even his eyesight seemed better in this splendid air, he thought.

A deep breath. And with that impetuosity which arises

14

from either complete lack of fear or pure terror he flung himself into the water.

He swam strongly out into the loch, then floated happily on his back for a few minutes, before returning to the bank with an easy back-stroke.

As he pulled himself out of the water, he felt something was wrong. The source of this feeling was easy to trace. Where there had been two boots there were now four.

Two of them were occupied by the young man in the bright tartan shirt.

His right hand was also occupied—by a small but efficient-looking pistol.

'Did no one ever tell you,' he said, 'how dangerous it is to swim alone?'

2

Professor James Nevis, OBE, DSO, MC (Bar), looked at the body in the water with some slight stirrings of distress.

His whole upbringing told him that it was positively indecent for a sixty-year-old man with grey hair and a hernia to enjoy the lightly covered contours of his twenty-five-year-old niece as he was doing at this moment. It was almost incestuous. But he could hardly ask her to start wearing voluminous gowns whenever he was around. Particularly not to swim in.

He hadn't really wanted a twenty-five-by-ten swimming pool in his back garden, but the house had been ideal and it had seemed silly to fill the damn' thing in. Besides, it had helped his image with the younger men in the faculty, who, despite their proletarian sympathies, always proved very keen to sample both his excellent wine and his chlorined water.

But he had not foreseen that his younger brother, domiciled in America for nearly thirty years, would have fathered such an attractive girl. Nor that she would have chosen the University of Lincoln as the place to complete her higher education. Nor that the English climate could have produced sunshine of such tropical intensity for so long.

Caroline Nevis opened her eyes and smiled up at him. 'Hi, James,' she said. The 'uncle' had been dropped by mutual consent soon after her arrival the previous October. Lazily, she paddled her hands in the water so that the air-bed on which she lay moved to the pool's edge.

'The post's here,' said Nevis, holding up an envelope. 'Your mother's handwriting.'

Caroline pushed herself upright, nearly lost her balance, but managed to steady herself with her legs astraddle the air-bed. Nevis found the change of position did not help.

'Thanks,' said the girl, taking the letter. 'Nothing from Bill?'

'No. I'm afraid not. He must be enjoying his holiday too much,' said Nevis neutrally. Caroline grinned at him. She knew he felt that his brother and sister-in-law might be a little piqued if she got into some sort of emotional tangle while under his roof. Particularly with a short, plump, balding, thirty-eight-year-old university Deputy Registrar.

She opened her letter and read it, amused as always by her mother's stilted, formal style. Her father, who had lived in America since 1946 and been an American citizen since 1950, always wrote with a breezy, chatty, unpunctuated casualness quite unlike his normal speech. But her mother, fourth-generation Californian, who moved in a flood of talk as overwhelming and as unstructured as Niagara, had been 'taught' correct letter-writing at an impressionable age and never got out of the habit.

'All well?' asked Nevis.

'Sure,' said Caroline. 'She's still talking about coming over.'

'And your father?'

'You know Daddy. He doesn't want to know about Europe.'

'Each to his taste,' said Nevis neutrally.

His brother John, five years his junior, had abandoned Europe in general and Britain in particular shortly after the end of the war. 'I did not fight for *this*,' he said, *this* ranging from the creation of communist Eastern Europe to Mr Attlee's Labour government. James, who had always found his brother a boringly solemn young man, was not much concerned to see him go. They disagreed about practically everything. Only the peculiar transatlantic respect for the title of professor could have convinced John he had become sufficiently stable to be entrusted with his daughter. Caroline had been a pleasant surprise, but Nevis had growing doubts about his wisdom in accepting the responsibility.

Caroline reached for the side of the pool and with a single easy movement pulled herself out of the water. Nevis again tried to feel avuncular as he admired her sun-browned frame—small, compact, but full of strength and grace. Not that she was an athlete. If she could just as easily ride somewhere as walk, she saw no reason not to choose comfort. It was a source of much contention between her and William Blake Hazlitt.

Exactly what she felt about him she was far from sure. But his sudden disappearance a week earlier had left a considerable gap in her life. She frowned now, realising that 'disappearance' had completely dislodged 'departure'.

There had been a phone call, breaking a date. Sorry, but a conference he was organising had been cancelled, leaving a fortnight's gap in his work schedule, and it seemed too good an opportunity to miss to take up some back vacation, so he was off on the night plane. . . . Where? she had asked. But the night plane, it seemed, would not stay for an answer.

That had been odd. Odder were the descriptions from common acquaintances in the university administration of the brutal suddenness with which Bill had made off, leaving stacks of work for others to cope with.

And oddest had been seven days' silence. Not a call, not a postcard.

'How's the thesis?' asked Nevis.

'So so. It needs a little structuring, I guess. There's just so much material.'

But her mind was not on the problem of Robert Southey's influence on the poetry of Walt Whitman which had been occupying her working hours for the past three years and which felt as if it might occupy them for the next three also.

Her mind was on the problem of William Blake Hazlitt. It was time she did something.

He must be in trouble.

And, boy, if he wasn't in trouble, was he in trouble!

The sun was warm on her shoulders. She looked longingly at the pool, but resisted the temptation to plunge back in.

There were much more important things to be done.

The Old Etonian had been born in a Huddersfield back-to-back and educated at the Mill Lane Charity School for the Children of the Destitute, whose ranks he might well have joined had not the Army's ranks been even more eager to claim him. Here low cunning, ruthlessness and the gift of mimicry proved the exact qualities needed for self-advancement, and the Special Operations Executive the best place to practise them in.

His new elevation had not ended with the war. Instead he found his talents in even greater demand, till finally he became a giver of orders rather than a taker. For so long now had he been living in his Sloane Street flat as an Old Etonian race-goer of independent means that he had practically forgotten his Yorkshire childhood.

In his flat there were two phones, one of which he always answered with great distaste. This was the one his team used for reporting in. Or for his masters checking up on him.

It rang now.

'Hello,' he said cautiously.

'This Hazlitt business. What's going on?'

The voice at the other end cultivated northern brusqueness as assiduously as the Old Etonian his own lengthened vowels.

'Pretty straightforward, sir. We made an approach, offered him a deal.'

'Which he accepted?'

'Well, not exactly. No; in a few words, no.'

'So you took him in.'

'Wrong again, I'm afraid, sir. He made a break for it, got clear away. But we're close to him now.'

'That'll be nice. You'll take him then?'

'Well, no, sir. You see, I think he may lead us to them, if you follow me.'

'Why not just thump it out of him?'

The Old Etonian sighed with distaste, remembering the old days when only gentlemen got to the top, with a few remarkable exceptions.

'I doubt if he'd talk, sir. It will be better this way, I assure you.'

'You'd best be right. What about Lincoln? Is that covered?'

'Yes, yes, rest assured. We're covering any likely contacts. There's an American girl he seems to have been interested in.'

'American, you say? We want no truck with the sodding Americans. You keep her out of this, do you hear? Make sure she stays clear.'

'Of course, sir. I'll put one of my best men on it.'

'You do that. Keep me posted. Right?'

The phone was thumped down. The Old Etonian shook his head, depressed the rest, dialled a number.

'Hello,' he said. 'Tell me, who's active in Lincoln just now. Who? Durban? Oh, I see. Well, I suppose he'll have to do. Tell him to fasten on to the girl. I want to know everything she does. Everything.'

Durban, he thought gloomily as he replaced the receiver. He had a sudden presentiment it was going to be a bad week.

Hazlitt idly splashed around in the water and wondered what the man in the tartan shirt proposed to do now. Not shoot him, it seemed. His mad, panic-stricken sprint away from the shore had brought no pursuing shots. It had been a stupid reaction brought on by violent scrotum-twisting fear. But it turned out to have been the right one.

The tartan-shirted man, whom Hazlitt now thought of as Tom (Mark II) as opposed to the probably wholly innocent Tom (Mark I) in the fawn raincoat, had not fired. Bullet holes caused talk. But Hazlitt was certain that, had he climbed out on to the bank, Tom (Mark II) would have found some undectable method of rendering him unconscious before returning his body to drown in the loch.

Tragic Accident on Skye. Two lines in the dailies.

Or some enterprising muck-raker caught short in the silly season might make a little more of it. *Nude Registrar Probe.* That was a nice come-on. *A police spokesman said that drowning while under the influence of drugs and attempting to have illicit intercourse with a cormorant was not suspected.*

If he couldn't be tragic, he might as well be titillating. But at the moment he saw no immediate need to be either. All he had to do was splash around in the middle of the loch for a couple of hours, which to a swimmer of his capacity was no problem. Then the afternoon boat would arrive, the trippers would appear over the ridge and Tom would be most reluctant to try anything nasty under the gaze of all those Japanese binoculars.

Idly he wondered what excuse Tom had made for wanting to be left alone till the boat returned. Bird-watching, perhaps. Or a sudden attack of pantheism. Whatever the reason, his fellow-travellers must have thought it odd of him to abandon his young bride.

He smiled at the thought of fellow-travellers. An out-moded term now, but still with lots of emotive power for the over-thirties. Some more than others.

Something splashed in the water not far from his face. A fish rising perhaps. He had by strictly illegal and un-sporting means supplemented his imported rations with a couple of fat trout during the past week.

Splosh.

No fish that. He trod water and peered short-sight-edly at the shore. At this distance outlines were blurred and Tom might have been a bright-shirted scarecrow with one arm outstretched.

Splosh. Splosh. Splosh.

A slow suspicion began to mature in Hazlitt's mind and he duck-dived in terror as the water spurted up in his face.

The scarecrow's arm was outstretched because he had a gun in it, which was presently pumping bullets into the unresentful loch. What had brought about this sud-den change in Tom's plans he couldn't guess. Perhaps the knowledge that he could not afford to wait till the boat returned. And while accidental death would have been preferred, at a pinch cold-blooded murder would have to do.

He surfaced for a quick bite of sun-flavoured air, but didn't stay for seconds. His mind registered that Tom must have fitted a silencer. Clever. There were always ears, even in so remote an area. Walkers, climbers; on a day like this, gun-shot sounds could carry for miles.

Which was more than could be said for bullets from such a small pistol, he reassured himself as he made land-fall on the opposite shore. He glanced back over the loch. Tom was still standing there. It would need a miracle for the man to hit his target at this range.

Hazlitt made a derisive gesture which, superstitiously, he immediately regretted. God was not mocked. It might be wise to hop out on the bank and increase the size of the required miracle by a few feet of solid rock.

Gingerly he clambered out, happy to feel the full heat of the sun once more. The waters of the loch had chilled him more than he realised. He stretched luxuriantly and turned his face upwards so that the sun filled his eyes. For a few moments after he looked away he could see nothing but a golden glow. After a while he began to see shapes again. And then he could see colour.

Last of all he turned round and saw why Tom's fellow-travellers had not thought it odd of him to abandon his young bride.

She was standing before him, looking remarkably like her 'husband'. Not only did their shirts match, so did their guns.

Perhaps she was as reluctant to use it. He would put it to the test.

With an apologetic smile, he grabbed for her arm. Somehow he missed by a mile and instead found his own arms seized, crossed, felt pressure applied, bent with it to prevent the bones breaking, and found himself float-ing gently through the summer-perfumed air.

He hit the ground with a crash that knocked all the breath out of his body. More than breath, he suspected. When he staggered to his feet again he half expected to see many vital internal organs scattered around.

The woman and the gun were before him once more. After vainglory, modesty is the most strongly con-ditioned reflex of the English. He found that, dazed

24

though he was, he was standing like a footballer facing a free kick, his hands crossed defensively over his crotch.

She made a gesture with the gun.

'Hands up,' she said.

Surprisingly, he found he was still able to laugh.

3

Caroline knew how a private eye worked. He slapped photos on bars and said out of the side of his mouth, 'Know him?' Or wore his shabby raincoat in the houses of the rich, was more than a match for their sneers, and finally provoked them into an admission of guilt.

But that was in California, USA. In Lincoln, England, things were different.

To start with, she hadn't got a photo. And at three o'clock in the afternoon there were no bars open to bang her non-photo down on. It wasn't the weather for shabby raincoats either, so she compromised with sun-top and slacks and started collecting sneers at Hazlitt's office.

Miss Plackett, his secretary, was totally unhelpful. Of an age with Hazlitt and twice his size, she had built up a substantial matrimonial fantasy based entirely on what might or might not have been a deliberate side-swipe of her left buttock at a Christmas party two years ago. Caroline (quite unconsciously) was her rival. Only constant self-reminders of her mother's dictum that little men liked big girls kept Miss Plackett's hopes alive.

She managed to imply totally fallaciously that she knew more than she cared to say and Caroline went away more worried than ever.

In a neighbouring office two very smooth young men, who were called administrative assistants and wanted (according to Hazlitt) Hazlitt's job, were drinking tea.

They greeted her with little cries of pleasure. They were called, unbelievably, Tarquin and Sholto, and Hazlitt tried to counter the feelings of inadequacy their youth and elegance gave him by pretending he could not distinguish between them.

Caroline had no such difficulty. Tarquin Adam was the one she had found in her uncle's pool late one night swimming naked with the Reader in Moral Philosophy. She had never mentioned this to Hazlitt, and Tarquin always greeted her conspiratorially, as though bent on advertising to the world that they shared a guilty secret.

Sholto Greig, on the other hand, who was the elder by about three years, presented quite another problem in that he had paid fervent court to her during her first few weeks at the university and had said some biting things about American father-fixations when she started seeing a great deal of Hazlitt.

But he was the more helpful of the two when she started making her casual, non-alarmist enquiries about Hazlitt's possible whereabouts.

'Not even a dirty postcard,' complained Tarquin. 'Mind you, duckie, we're not entirely surprised, I can tell you. Oh no. The poor chap's been abrogating his responsibilities for some time now. No paper in the gents', waste-paper baskets not emptied, lipstick on the coffee-cups. We've been positively carrying him for months, you know.'

Sholto took her arm and led her away into another office.

'You're not really worried, are you?'

'Yes. Well, to tell you the truth, I am, just a bit. It's not like him, going off like this. At least I don't think it's like him. I haven't known him all that long, I guess.'

Sholto's thin, finely-boned face creased in sympathy.

'You're right,' he assured her, adding reluctantly,

28

'Tarquin's a fool, I know, but there's just a bit of truth in what he says. Bill has been a bit edgy of late. It's nothing at the office, I'm sure. I even thought it might have something to do with . . .'

He tailed off. Caroline shook her head.

'No. Nothing to do with me. At least I don't think so. I noticed it too.'

'Look,' said Sholto, 'would you like to speak to Stuart?'

Caroline hesitated. Stewart Stuart, the Registrar, was a man who intimidated her considerably. His physical bulk was bad enough, but it was his manner, perfected and refined during thirty years of distinguished service in Whitehall, that bothered her most. Nothing seemed to be done without forethought. Even his absurdities seemed as well organised as a grandmaster's moves in a chess match. Sir Walter Tyas, the erstwhile Cabinet Minister, disappointed in his hopes of the party leadership eight years earlier, had soon afterwards slipped gracefully out of political life and become Vice-Chancellor of Lincoln. With him from the corridors of power he had brought Stuart. Together they had re-organised ramshackle structures and raised standards to a pitch where Sir Walter could claim that Lincoln University was perhaps the only one in the country which could guarantee the literacy of all its students.

Hazlitt had assisted with this work for six years now, too long career-wise, but with an unspoken promise that when Stuart retired in a couple of years the job would fall into his lap. He and the Registrar had a good working relationship and shared a taste for excellence in food and wine. Sometimes Caroline felt herself cut out by the two of them together and memory of this made her shake her head now.

'Later perhaps,' she said.

'I wish you would,' said Sholto. 'There's this African

trip coming off soon and Bill really ought to be here making sure his work's organised.'

'Okay. Thanks, Sholto,' said Caroline.

Thanks for what? she wondered. She was leaving the registry even more worried than when she had arrived. The African trip referred to was only five weeks away and its proximity certainly made Hazlitt's behaviour even more difficult to understand. He had been invited to be the Acting Registrar of the new African University of Balowa for a six-month period. He had been out there in an advisory capacity some eighteen months earlier and had done an excellent job. While out there he had renewed the acquaintance of George Oto (now Colonel Oto), whom he had known vaguely at Oxford. Now after a sudden but bloodless change of government Oto was Premier and he personally had issued the invitation to Hazlitt, making the whole business still more prestigious.

This was certainly something Hazlitt would not want to mess up. Perhaps, thought Caroline suddenly, perhaps that was where he had gone. Africa. But why?

Hell, it was just a wild guess, she told herself angrily, leaving the university. Let's go and get some facts.

Next stop was Hazlitt's flat. He insisted on living centrally, a necessity, since he had foresworn cars some years earlier and did not wish to be a slave of the bus service. He sometimes rode an enormous bicycle, but a few spots of rain on his thick glasses turned him into a pavement-mounting, policeman-bashing menace.

The bike stood in the entrance hall like the centrepiece of an industrial museum. Mrs Searle, Hazlitt's landlady, who lived in the basement, had opened the door for Caroline, who now stood alone in the lounge and wondered what she was looking for.

She had only been here four or five times before. On none of these occasions had there been any suggestion that she might stay all night which had slightly disappointed Caroline. She was not a girl who slept around, but she was used to the company of young men who would rapidly and persuasively make the suggestion.

The worrying thought that Hazlitt's interest might not be developing at the same pace as her own occurred again. She was not really certain if she had any right to feel so concerned about him. But she was here now and to leave without looking would be stupid.

Five minutes later she was ready to give up. Her fears were stupid, she decided. For whatever reason, Hazlitt had wanted to get away for a few days. Why shouldn't he? He was a mature man. Too mature, perhaps. Why involve a mere slip of a girl in your business?

She looked at herself in the mirror.

'Bullshit,' she said aloud. Small she might be, but definitely not a mere slip of a girl. She went through into the bedroom and began opening drawers.

Half a minute later she found his passport. Its significance escaped her for a moment, then it dawned. Wherever else Hazlitt was, he was not in Africa. Or anywhere out of the country.

She opened the wardrobe. Not having known the man for a full round of the seasons, her acquaintance with his clothes was incomplete, so what had been taken was difficult to say. She recognised his two well-cut office suits, made by a Bradford tailor, visits to whom saved Hazlitt twenty pounds a time, or so he claimed, and also made him the best-dressed man in the senior common room. It was one of his dearest affectations. He had been genuinely hurt when Caroline suggested they were from C and A with the labels cut out.

In for a penny, she thought, and went through the pockets. He was a great collector of rubbish; all the litter of a hypochondriac was there: indigestion tablets in silver foil, throat lozenges, bits of Elastoplast; plus restaurant bills going back for eighteen months, bus and train tickets, pieces of newspaper, shop receipts.

These last caught her eye because of their comparative newness. She looked more closely and found they were all from Enoch Arden's, the big departmental store in the city centre. The date on them was the day before his departure. And the one or two items she could decipher made her think deeply.

Nothing else turned up, so she headed for Enoch Arden's, pausing only to tell Mrs Searle she was finished.

The old woman, who had accepted Caroline's lame excuse for wanting to enter the flat with unprotesting incredulity, took back the key in silence.

'You've no idea when Mr Hazlitt's coming back?' asked Caroline unhopefully.

'None,' said Mrs Searle, shaking her head emphatically.

'Or where he's gone?'

The woman busied herself with rearranging a vase full of long dead chrysanthemums.

'None,' she repeated with much less emphasis.

Caroline sensed an evasion, perhaps even a lie, but Mrs Searle retreated to her pop-filled kitchen, bringing the interview to an end. Worth another try later, thought Caroline, after she'd thought out her tactics. Meanwhile there was Enoch Arden's.

It was a good store as provincial shops go. Everyone was most helpful, readily accepting her story of wanting to check that all the items her friend had bought had reached home safely. She was amazed to find that some of the clothing items had been purchased in the children's department. These were clearly advantages in having small feet!

Most of the stuff, however, came from Sport and Outdoors in the basement. And there was no doubt about the significance of the complete list. Hazlitt had been planning to go on a camping trip. The realisation surprised her. Hazlitt was a keen walker, she knew. And had in the past been a lover of tents and all that went with them. But that was in his youth, he had jokingly told her. He joked rather too frequently about his lost youth.

She looked at the list again. It was a stocking-up list, not a basic outfitting list. The big items—tent, rucksack, sleeping bag, etc.—were missing. Hazlitt would own these already. But there had been no sign of them in her search of his flat.

She felt she was getting somewhere, but did not quite know where. At least everything so far pointed to a departure from choice. She glanced at her watch. Time for a cup of tea, then back to see what Mrs Searle really knew. She made for the restaurant.

A worried-looking young man with flaxen hair crouched in the telephone booth.

'Hello, hello. Is that Superstar? Goblin speaking.'

'Who?' asked a languid Old Etonian voice.

'Goblin.'

'Yes, I can hear you are. But who are you?'

'Well, its Durban, sir,' whispered Durban.

'Why are you whispering, man? Speak up.'

'DURBAN!'

'Ah,' said the Old Etonian. 'Hold on. There we are.'

'Are you scrambling, sir?' asked Durban hopefully.

'With you, Durban, who needs a scrambler? No, I'm merely taking one of my pills. What do you want?'

'It's the girl, sir. She's been to the registry. Then to the landlady's. And now she's been wandering round this shop . . .'

'Shop? You're in a shop?'

'Yes. Enoch Arden's, a big departmental store.'

'I see. Really, Durban, I'm not interested in the

minutiae of the girl's everyday life.'

'No, sir. But she's been asking about camping gear. Stuff *he* bought.'

'I see,' said the Old Etonian slowly. 'Can hardly mean anything. Still, we don't want her around, do we?'

'She's a bright girl, sir.'

'Yes, these Americans have a certain animal instinct for the chase. It's all this frontier survival thing, I suppose. You say she's still in the shop?'

'Yes, sir. Drinking tea.'

'Splendid. I think we'd better immobilise her just to be on the safe side. Yes, yes, I think we had better. My dear fellow, if only you knew the decisions I have to make!'

The Old Etonian replaced the phone, went through into his kitchen and ground some coffee beans. His presentiment seemed to have been justified. It was turning into a terrible week.

Caroline finished her tea, unhooked her capacious shoulder bag from over the back of her chair and rode the escalator to the ground floor. She was suddenly imbued with confidence that all was going well, discoveries had been and were about to be made. This private-eye business was kid's play to an intelligent girl. She approached the store's main exit.

A tall woman stood between her and the door.

'Excuse me,' said Caroline.

The woman didn't move.

'Will you please accompany me to the manager's office?' she said.

'Sorry?' said Caroline, puzzled.

A rather embarrassed-looking young man joined the woman.

'This way, please,' he said with a slight stutter.

Some kind of demonstration? Caroline wondered.

34

'No thanks,' she said. 'Some other time, huh?'

'Let's not have a public scene, madam,' said the tall woman patronisingly. 'Just come this way.'

She was very efficient. The hand that appeared to light gently on Caroline's elbow gripped like a vice and she found herself being moved rapidly through Perfumerie and Handbags to a small office by the lift.

An older man was sitting at a desk. She vaguely recognised him as the store manager from seeing him distantly in the shop.

'What the hell is this?' she demanded.

'Have you purchased any goods in the shop today, madam?' he asked.

'No, and I'm not likely to again if I don't get a pretty fast explanation!'

'Would you please show us what you have in your shoulder bag?' said the manager.

Slowly Caroline slid her mini-duffel bag off her shoulder. She was a tidy person and knew exactly the half-dozen or so items it contained.

But a part of her mind other than the conscious and rational level was beginning to know different.

And it hardly came as any surprise to her to look down and see the handsome silver bracelet which gleamed accusingly from the depths of her bag.

It came as a great surprise to Hazlitt that he was still alive half an hour after being caught by the girl. Or rather the woman. Close up, she turned out to be far from the blushing bride of his earlier imaginings. She was in her thirties, rather plain, and exuding a most sinister competence.

He tried to talk with her as she shepherded him round the loch, but the only reply he got was a painful jab at the base of his spine when he did not move fast enough. By the time they reached the recumbent Tom, Hazlitt was sweating copiously. The only thing which had kept him alive was the desirability of making his death look accidental, of this he was sure. But he felt no urge to take to the water again. Last time, Tom (Mark II) had known he could get him back once the woman was in place. This time, with no back-stop, they might not be so patient but make do with a bullet through his head.

'Welcome back,' said Tom. 'Enjoy your swim?'

He had a line in facetiousness which Hazlitt found particularly distressing. The woman didn't seem to care for it either.

'Let's get it done,' she said sharply. 'There's not much time.'

Suddenly he preferred Tom's facetiousness.

'Listen,' he said urgently. 'Do you know what you're doing? What have they told you?'

'Will you do it, my dear Cherry, or shall I?' asked Tom with mock courtesy.

'Just get on with it,' said the woman.

If there was any hope, Hazlitt realised, it lay with the woman. Tom was getting kicks out of the situation. Any pleas he could make would merely increase his pleasure. The woman's cold efficiency was purely professional. There was nothing in it for her personally. And she had a name. Cherry. A nice name. You couldn't be a *killer* with a name like Cherry.

He realised Tom was trying to get behind him and he began to back away. He had to keep both of them in sight as long as possible. His mind desperately sought for something he could say which might at least make the woman hesitate. This was not a moment for truth. Anybody could tell the truth and get killed for it.

'Stand still or I'll shoot your knee-cap off!' commanded Tom.

'Can't we talk this thing out?' asked Hazlitt, retreating from the loch side and walking backwards up the ghyll in which his tent was pitched. He found it difficult to walk backwards, but he was certainly not going to turn his back on them.

'Do you know what's going on?' he demanded of the woman. 'Do you know who I am?'

'Hurry up,' said the woman to Tom. 'I'd like to get home tonight.'

'I'm a married man,' proclaimed Hazlitt. 'I have a wife and several children. What will they do without a father? Surely you can understand that.'

He looked appealingly at the woman.

'I'm a widow,' she answered. 'I manage very well. You're just dragging things out.'

'Let him talk,' grinned Tom, producing from his pocket a broad roll of some kind of gauze. What its function was, Hazlitt did not know, but he was not at all eager to find out.

'I'm completely innocent,' he said. 'All I want is a chance to state my case. That's all. You can't refuse me that.'

'All right,' said Tom. 'Come down here and let's talk it over.'

'Oh no,' said Hazlitt. 'No. I'll go back with you on the boat, how about that?'

'Now that would be very nice,' said Tom. 'Except that you don't have a ticket.'

He jumped forward. Hazlitt scuttled backwards in panic, trod on a jagged edge of rock, jerked his naked foot away and fell.

Tom was on him like a cat, forcing his arms behind his back with a violence that made him scream. Struggle merely increased the pain, so he lay still, his eyes full of involuntary tears, while the man bound the white gauze round his wrists. It was, he realised, self-adhesive bandage. Its advantages were obvious. His limbs could be bound fast. No matter how hard he struggled, unlike rope the broad binding would leave no telltale burns. And no matter how tight it was applied, unlike tape it would not bring away any skin or hair when removed.

Tom was now wrapping the bandage round his legs, binding them together the whole length of the calf. Strength seemed to have left his body and the will to resist his mind. He lay still and felt the hands of his murderer move caressingly over his thigh. Now he looked into the man's face. And what he saw there made him give up hope.

Now he was over Tom's shoulders in a fireman's lift and being borne rapidly back towards the loch. The plan was clear. Drop him in, leave him there for ten minutes, pull him out, remove the bandages, then push him back in and you have your perfect accidental drowning.

The world spun crazily round his upside-down head, he felt sick, images of his life began to coalesce in his mind. Tom halted on the bank.

'God bless this body,' he said, 'and all who sail on it.'

'Please,' begged Hazlitt. 'Please. There's no need for this, I promise you.'

'Wait,' said the woman.

A spark of hope glowed bright in Hazlitt's mind.

The woman stepped forward, tried the bandage round his wrists and nodded her satisfaction.

'Okay,' she said.

Next moment he was hurtling through the air and the brackish waters of the loch stifled back his cry of protest.

4

Everyone was being so sympathetic that Caroline felt sick.

As this was the condition which everyone seemed bent on assuming she was in, all that happened was more sympathy. The store manager fetched glasses of water and the police. The police asked if she had been unwell recently, slanderously hinting at the imminence of her menopause. Her uncle, Professor Nevis, appeared after half an hour and offered to summon her doctor.

All present nodded their heads sagely at the mention of the doctor.

'I am not ill!' snapped Caroline. 'Listen, you Lieutenant or whatever you are . . .'

'Inspector Servis, miss.'

'. . . all right, Inspector, I don't know who and I don't know why, but someone planted that thing in my bag.'

She pointed dramatically at the silver bracelet which gleamed accusingly on the manager's desk.

'You *were* in the jewellery department?' said the Inspector.

'No! Well, I may have passed through on my way somewhere else.'

The tall woman spoke. Her name was Miss Park and she was a store detective.

'A young man informed one of the assistants that he

believed he had observed a woman removing a bracelet from a display in Jewellery. The description he gave fitted Miss Nevis, whom I observed sitting at a table in our restaurant. I left someone to watch her and checked her movements in the store. This proved fairly easy, as her behaviour had drawn some attention. She was going around with old receipts checking on the items represented by the stock numbers entered there.'

'So what?' said Caroline. 'Why should I draw attention to myself? And where's this young man who put the finger on me?'

'As you will know from your work, Inspector, witnesses are frequently reluctant to become involved. The young man did not leave his name. However, I felt I had sufficient to work on, a check with Jewellery having revealed a bracelet to be missing, so I went to the main entrance and apprehended Miss Nevis as she tried to leave.'

'Tried to leave!' exploded Caroline. 'You make it sound like a break-out!'

In one corner of the room Professor Nevis was talking persuasively to the manager. Caroline subsided in time to get the tail-end of their conversation.

'It's not up to me, sir,' said the manager. 'Our general policy is to prosecute. I'll have to consult the chairman.'

'Please do that,' said Nevis. 'I'll have a word with him myself. Now I wonder if I could take my niece home?'

'Well, sir?' said the inspector to the manager.

'Look, I'm not sure whether we'll want to prosecute or not. I'd like time to talk to my employers.'

Servis looked doubtful.

'It's not usual,' he mused. 'Still, in the circumstances, and as Miss Nevis is a foreign national, perhaps we could leave the decision in abeyance for a while. Miss Nevis, you must understand that this investigation is still proceeding and you must make yourself available for further questioning. You will be remaining in Lincoln for the next few days?'

'Yes. I'll vouch for that,' answered Nevis, shaking his head sternly at Caroline's attempted protest.

'In that case,' said the inspector, opening the door, 'I would have that word with the young lady's doctor, sir. A professional opinion's always worth while.'

With difficulty Caroline restrained herself from striking him. Shaking with anger, she stuffed her belongings back in her bag.

'I can still *walk* by myself, James,' she snapped at the professor, who offered her the support of his arm as they left the shop.

'Of course, my dear,' he answered. 'My car's over the road. Let's go home and have a couple of stiff ones, shall we?'

She glared at him in exasperation and wondered if anyone had ever been driven to murder by a surfeit of kindness.

'No, you go on,' she answered. 'I've got some books to pick up at the university library. I'll probably work there for a couple of hours.'

She walked quickly away before he could raise any objections. When she glanced back after fifty yards or so he was still standing on the pavement, tall, distinguished and worried, gazing after her. It made her feel guilty and she almost went back to him. Instead she raised a hand in greeting and went on her way. So busy were her thoughts that it did not occur to her to wonder as she glanced back why the flaxen-haired man with the newspaper protruding from his pocket should have felt it necessary to halt and purchase another from the kerbside vendor.

Hazlitt managed to get himself back within a yard of the shore, but with Tom (Mark II) standing there it might as well have been a mile. There is a limit to the amount of time even an expert swimmer can keep afloat with his arms and legs securely bound. Paradoxically the experience of being drowned tends to stretch out this time rather than shorten it. Seconds swell to minutes and a minute can hold enough pain and fear to curdle a lifetime.

Traditionally a man's whole past flashes across the inward eye in such circumstances. Hazlitt kept the past out, refused to look, tried instead to reach for a future which included him alive and well and living in Leamington Spa. Or Luton. Or even Llandudno. Yes, he would willingly accept such dreadful exile. But God was in no mood for making bargains and at last the pictures started to flicker. Mercifully they were all good pictures —himself aged nine reading *Wind in the Willows* for the first time; the letter bearing news of his university scholarship; the exquisite niggle with which he won the JCR shove-half-penny competition; the bottle of Château Pavie '55 which he had thought of keeping for another year but which, God be praised, he had drunk on his last birthday; and, last of all, the face of a girl, in theory all he hated most in women, young, bright, pert, voluble, American, but now last and best in his mind before the lights went out and all pictures faded into utter darkness.

Stewart Stuart, the university Registrar, was a large man, quite impassable when he stood as he did now in the centre of one of the aisles in the library.

Caroline's claimed destination had merely been a lie to get herself away from Professor Nevis, but on further reflection if had appeared a good place to go and have a quiet brood on recent events.

'Well, Miss Nevis, hello!'

His voice had the volume of a large man's but none

of the jolliness. The Scottishness suggested by his name was completely absent. Caroline supposed the name itself was some ghastly parental practical joke. A female dwarf librarian appeared at the end of the aisle and looked at them reprovingly.

'Well hello!' repeated Stuart. Repetition was a feature of his public oratorical style. And of his work methods, so his underlings asserted. 'Where's Hazlitt? Eh? That's the question. Where's Hazlitt?'

'Sh!' said the dwarf librarian. 'Over there. 820.4, Literary Criticism, English.'

'No. Not *that* Hazlitt. Not that Hazlitt. William Blake Hazlitt, I mean. Foolish woman!'

He shook his head ferociously at the dwarf librarian, who retreated saying, 'Blake 821, English Poets. To your left,' till she and her voice disappeared at the same time.

'I'm afraid I don't know,' said Caroline.

'Don't *know*? *Don't* know?' said Stuart, varying the stress meaninglessly. 'What *I* think is, what I *think* is . . . not possible. No.'

'What do you think?'

'What *I* think *is* . . . Poulson! What do *you* think?'

A rather grey young man who had appeared moment-arily at some distance looked round in surprise at being hailed as though on the open sea. He was Thomas Poulson, lecturer in the Law Department, and Hazlitt's favourite squash opponent, as his tendency to sudden fits of abstraction made him easily beatable.

He approached cautiously.

'Yes?' he said. 'What is it you want, Stuart?'

Caroline tried to work out whether the Registrar was being addressed familiarly by his Christian name or for-mally by his surname.

'Have you heard from Hazlitt?'

Poulson ingested the question slowly.

'No,' he said finally.

43

'There!' said Stuart triumphantly. 'There! And Africa are on the phone all the time.'

'Oh, are it?' said Poulson. Caroline giggled.

'Someone's got to work,' said Stuart, and strode purposefully away.

'What's he doing in the library?' wondered Poulson.

'You're a bit off the beaten track yourself,' said Caroline.

'Oh, hello, Caroline,' said Poulson, as though noticing her for the first time. 'I'm after thrillers. Do you have thrillers?'

'From time to time,' said Caroline. 'You mean books?'

'Yes. They always get their law wrong, you see. I thought they might provide some interesting seminar problems.'

'Thomas,' said Caroline, 'do you have a moment? I have an interesting seminar problem.'

She drew him into a working alcove and they sat down. At first her intention was merely to pour her worries about Hazlitt into a friendly ear, but it struck her suddenly that only fools and saints didn't abuse their friendship with lawyers. Quickly she told him what had happened in Enoch Arden's that day.

'An inspector, you say?' said Poulson.

'That's right.'

'It was a valuable bracelet?'

'Hell no! I mean, not your Liz Taylor bit. Twenty, maybe twenty-five dollars. Sorry, ten pounds at the most.'

'And no charge. Not yet. But this inspector told you to keep yourself available for the next few days. Did he take a statement?'

'If you mean, did I sign anything, the answer's no. Just told me not to leave town.'

'Odd,' said Poulson, and, bending his head, seemed to concentrate all his attention on the words *Shakespeare was a nut* which some earnest student had inscribed in

44

pencil on the table-top. Caroline recognised the fit of abstraction, sighed, rose, made her way to the nearest shelves, and selected a book at random. It was wedged firmly between its two neighbours and she had to pull hard to get it out. Too hard. A large tome of Coleridge's activities as a French agent came with it and hit the ground explosively. The dwarf librarian appeared instantly and glared down the aisle. Behind her, legs aggressively astride like a marshal in a Western, was a blond young man with a newspaper in either jacket pocket and his hand reaching for his wallet.

Caroline shrugged expressively, replaced the book and, noticing signs of revival in Poulson, returned to the table.

'What's odd?' she asked.

'Presumably,' he said, 'you are even more ignorant of the workings of our legal system than most native citizens? So the oddities may have escaped you . . . It's odd that you were not charged, odd that this young man should have disappeared, it's odd that no other witness to your presence in the jewellery department was produced, it's odd that a man of the rank of inspector should investigate such a trifling matter, it's odd that you were not taken to the station, and it's odd that in the midst of all this solicitude which was coming your way no one thought to suggest you might send for a solicitor.'

'I see,' said Caroline. 'So all that's odd, huh?'

'No single matter is excessively odd, perhaps,' said Poulson. 'But the sum of effects is one of oddity.'

'And your explanation?'

He smiled and rose.

'Lawyers don't explain. They merely demonstrate. I must go now. Should you catch up with Hazlitt, ask him if our game is on next Wednesday. He didn't turn up last week. Goodbye, Caroline.'

45

He disappeared into the maze of shelves. After a moment Caroline rose too and made for the exit where the dwarf librarian scanned her closely, as though suspecting she had the complete works of Dickens concealed beneath her sun-top.

'*Ciao!*' said Caroline with a smile.

'636.71, Dogs,' the dwarf librarian called after her.

Hazlitt opened his eyes a few moments before breaking the surface skin of full consciousness. There was a heavy weight on his chest and he was surrounded by a dim religious light. The two things together made him wonder nightmarishly if he might be lying in state somewhere, with a heavy catafalque lid drawn back to reveal his farewell face. He was at a loss as to which country might have accorded him this honour, then his mind thrust up violently through the surface skin and he was awake.

He was in the land of the living and the dim religious light was merely sunshine filtered through the nylon eaves of his tent.

Without his spectacles, everything was very hazy. Somewhere close in the tent something grunted, an angry animal grunt, and the weight on his chest shifted slightly.

It was alive! He stiffened in panic, uncertain whether rapid movement or complete stillness were called for. Snake? Not in Skye, not this heavy. What then? Fox? Surely not. Wildcat? They still survived in Scotland, didn't they? Or perhaps it was merely a sociable sheep.

Slowly he raised an exploratory hand. He found himself grasping something round and warm and soft, pressure on which increased the creature's agitation tenfold.

He sat up abruptly and as he did so his glasses fell down from his forehead on to his nose. Someone had been very thoughtful.

Thoughtful indeed, he realised. Almost Oriental in

thought, having left him a half-naked woman conveniently bound and gagged.

She stared at him with antagonism and fear in her eyes.
He smiled reassuringly at her, wondering whether he
should apologise for his recent accidental attack on her
scantily covered bosom. But then it dawned on him that
perhaps even more reassuring to her would be the covering of his own naked frailties.

As he pulled on his spare trousers, he took stock of the
situation.

The woman, he now realised, was Cherry. The reason
for her lack of clothing above the waist was that someone had removed her tartan shirt and torn it into strips
wherewith to gag and bind her.

He looked around the tent but could see no sign of
her gun. Not that he would have very much idea what
to do with a gun even if he found one. But Cherry in
here did not necessarily mean that Tom (Mark II) was
not out there and some form of defence would be a comfort.

Still, it was pointless delaying investigation any
longer, so with another apologetic smile for the woman
as he rolled her to one side, he opened the tent flap and
cautiously poked his head out into the open air.

He instantly wished he hadn't.

Inside the tent had been the world of the living to
which he had been miraculously returned.

Out here it was the world of the dead. Sprawled out
on the heathery slope before him, as though taking his
ease in the sun, was Tom. Only it was an eternal ease.
All life must have instantly spilled through the large hole
in his chest.

Hazlitt sat down heavily and assessed the situation. At
least he put on the assessing-the-situation face he normally saved for those moments in Senate meetings when
he was unexpectedly invited to comment on some matter

47

of which he was completely ignorant. Inside there was nothing but confusion, centred upon a small but growing area of nausea in the pit of his stomach.

Outwardly, very little had changed. The loch, the mountains, and the sky were all in place. The sun scarcely seemed to have shifted its position. Not many minutes could have elapsed since Tom had hurled him into the water.

Tom. He raised his reluctant eyes and looked at him again. Things had certainly changed for Tom, the biggest change of all.

It was time for rational thought. His mind considered the possibilities and came up grasping the nub of the situation, the first and essential course of action.

He must finish getting dressed.

Whatever lay ahead of him, he would at least face it like an English gentleman.

The thought cheered him, but as he pulled on his tee-shirt and woolly socks other thoughts soon dispelled the cheer. For a start, whoever shot Tom was still around, alive and potentially lethal.

But, he assured himself, whoever shot Tom saved my life, is therefore my friend.

On the other hand, he answered, lacing up his walking boots, this 'friend' has left me with a corpse to explain. Not to mention a captive woman in my tent!

He crawled back inside and removed her gag. She breathed deeply but said nothing.

'You know he's dead?' he asked, reluctant to let her experience the same shock as he had done. She nodded.

'Who did it?' he asked.

She laughed scornfully.

'Someone up there loves you,' she said.

'That's nice. But why? And you. What have I done to you?'

'Me? Nothing. All I want to do is get back home.

48

Look, won't you loosen these bonds a bit? They're killing me.'

He looked thoughtfully at her. She was hog-tied, wrists and ankles pulled close together. Someone had been very efficient. But he did nothing and instead started packing.

Danger felt very close. Skye had seemed the ideal refuge in time of trouble, but now he was very aware that despite the lonely vastness of the mountains which lay about him, Skye was only a very small island, which could serve just as easily for a trap as a haven.

He pulled the woman out of the tent and noticed that she kept her eyes averted from the corpse. Quickly he struck camp, eager to be on his way now. At one point he paused, imagining he could hear the faint sea-changed chatter of an outboard motor, but decided it was probably just the distant call of a ptarmigan.

His last act was to take a small knife out of his camper's canteen and lay it on a stone some twenty yards downhill from the woman. He then released the piece of binding which held her ankles and her wrists together.

'Now,' he told her, 'you should be able to move pretty easily. Down there's a knife. A good half-hour's effort should get you to it and you can start cutting. I'd let you loose now, only you'd probably knock me down or give me a karate chop or something.'

'Thanks,' she said. He could not gauge the degree of her sincerity.

'I'm sorry. It's the best I can do. What you do with . . . him . . . well, that's up to you.'

'They'll get you in the end. You know that?' she said.

He shrugged but did not answer, hoisted his rucksack on his shoulders and set off up the lochside away from the sea.

5

'Scotland!' exclaimed Caroline.

'That's right,' said Mrs Searle.

'Why didn't you say so before?'

'Well, he just let it slip, by accident like, and made me promise not to tell anyone. But in the circumstances, well . . .'

'The circumstances' were that Caroline by sighs and blushes and innuendo had contrived to suggest to Mrs Searle's soap-operatic mind that Hazlitt had left her in the family way and that it was a matter of some urgency that she contacted him.

'And did you?'

'What?'

'Tell anyone.'

'No. Certainly not. I wouldn't!'

'Of course not,' said Caroline, certain the woman was lying. 'But someone did ask, didn't they?'

'Yes,' admitted Mrs Searle, glancing at the clock. It was nearly time for the second episode of her twice-weekly evening serial.

'Who?' asked Caroline, glancing at her own watch. She had returned home briefly and sat in her room for a while, contemplating the events of the day and trying to reach a conclusion other than that they had something to with Hazlitt's disappearance. But nothing else fitted, and the only untapped source of information that remained had been Mrs Searle. So just before dinner she had slipped out, allegedly to post a letter. Why she felt it necessary to lie to Professor Nevis she did not know. But last time she had proposed to return to Mrs Searle's had been from Enoch Arden's and that attempt had met with little success.

'Why? I don't know,' asserted Mrs Searle. 'Said they were friends.'

She stood up, went across to the television set and switched it on. Caroline also rose, recognising the interview was at an end. It was time she went home in any case. She had been gone too long already.

It was a fine summer evening, but she paid little heed to it as she hurried along the pavement. Her mind was trying to make sense of the whole affair. Only one thing was clear. Unease about Hazlitt had started her enquiries into his whereabouts, and nothing had happened to make her any less uneasy.

But the business in Enoch Arden's couldn't possibly have anything to do with it, could it? Not in England? Not in provincial England which was still so like the green, pleasant, quiet, well-ordered land her father described in his rare nostalgic moments. A frame-up *here*? It was impossible. A mistake, soon to be sorted out.

Her uncle was waiting for her in the dining room. He had not yet started to eat, though plainly the food had been on the table for some time.

'Sorry I'm late,' said Caroline.

He looked at her with an expression which seemed to combine sympathy and assessment. She could not interpret it clearly, in fact found it difficult to interpret much about her uncle very clearly. Perhaps it was because his subject—molecular biology—was so far removed from her own discipline. Perhaps it was because he was so completely different from his brother John, her father, whose blunt, uncompromising, rather naive view of life permitted few complexities of relationship. Caroline knew the brothers had quarrelled, or at least parted hastily, after the war and she felt her own presence here was symbolic of some kind of reconciliation. One which would hardly last if her father got wind of her present spot of bother. Not that it really worried her. Surely it would go no further.

'Caroline,' said her uncle, speaking with uncharacteristic abruptness, 'I'm sorry, but the police have just called. The store is going to prosecute, after all. You're to appear in court the day after tomorrow.'

'Oh my God,' said Caroline.

The Old Etonian was in the kitchen when the telephone rang.

'Smithson here, sir.'

'Hello, Smithson. What do they do with their telephone lines up there—float them down to Glasgow?'

'I'm sorry it's a bad line, sir.'

'Yes, all right. Well, why has my day been interrupted?'

'Just a report, sir. He's definitely there.'

'Splendid. It's always nice to be right.'

'Yes, sir. He's got company now.'

'Really? Us or them?'

'Both, sir.'

'That's all right, then.'

'Anything new at your end, sir?'

'My end is my own business, I think, Smithson. You might essay a polite laugh sometimes, you know. Durban seems to have been effective for once in his life and the girl has been taken out. Merely a precaution, of course, but they do possess a certain tenacity of purpose these Americans. Like beagles. Now, which way will Hazlitt break, do you think?'

'No idea, sir. And I'm out of contact temporarily.'

'Nothing wrong?'

'No, it's just the nature of the terrain. I should hear something pretty soon.'

'Where then? South or north? South would be nice.'

'Yes, but I doubt it. I think it could be a long job. He knows the country well.'

'I'm pleased. I shouldn't like anything to happen to him. Not yet. Not just yet.'

This is absurd, thought Hazlitt. I know the country well. I'm by way of being an expert. Besides which, I have had my share of troubles for today. This can't be happening.

He looked up at the gnarled and beautiful clumps of heather which his white knuckled hands were grasping, then down at the sharp boulders waiting at the foot of the sixty-foot drop over which his legs were dangling. With a shudder he closed his eyes. It was certainly happening.

His only previous acquaintance with the strength of heather had been in his vain attempts to force an errant golf ball out of it. (He was an abominable golfer. Not even Poulson at his most distracted ever lost to him.) Then he had cursed the stuff roundly. Now he blessed it as he tried to inch his way upward to the rocky crest on which he had missed his footing a few moments earlier.

It reacted badly to the blessing. The root he was holding with his right hand suddenly gave way and he slipped sideways as he scrabbled for a new hold, babbling a prayer to the god of the mountains.

It was answered immediately and, as might have been expected, by a Scottish deity.

> *'And here's a hand, my trusty fiere,*
> *And gie's a haud o'thine,'*

sang a flat but powerful baritone voice, a hand grasped his wrist and Hazlitt found himself being hauled effortlessly upwards. Safe on the crest, he collapsed in a langour of relief at the foot of his rescuer, who at first glance appeared to be a bearded lady of gigantic proportions.

He adjusted his glasses and the woman turned into a kilted Scotsman, booted and haversacked for the mountains. The proportions remained gigantic.

'Thanks,' said Hazlitt, rising unsteadily to his feet.

'Are you lost, then?'

The voice was educated Scottish, very deep and faintly mocking. There was a glimmer of white teeth through the black tangle of facial hair, as though the man were smiling.

'No!' protested Hazlitt, his pride stung. 'I know exactly where I am. I merely lost my footing.'

The man laughed loudly. Then he stuck out his hand and clasped Hazlitt's again.

'Lackie Campbell,' he said. 'If you're heading up the glen, I'll walk with you a ways.'

'Bill Hazlitt,' said Hazlitt. 'By all means. I'll be happy to show you the way.'

Campbell roared with laughter and waved Hazlitt in front of him, a position he accepted with some uneasiness. In his present state of mind he felt reluctant to expose his back to anyone, even to a man who had just saved him from possible serious injury. But the track they were following was too narrow for anything but single file and he had volunteered to lead. It was not the first time his hastiness had put him in undesirable positions. In fact, the whole business of coming to Skye which until a few hours ago had seemed so well planned and carefully executed now began to feel ill-conceived and bungled. He had long ago grown used to living within small capsules of time, bounded by the next pleasurable experience—a fine meal, a good play, a holiday in the hills and recently more and more often, a meeting with Caroline—but suddenly his present capsule had no such sensuous limits and all that he could conceive of outside it was a terrifying and unlimited emptiness.

As they descended towards the shining thread of water running through Glen Sligachan he stumbled once more and once more felt the big Scotsman's hand steadying him. It provoked another outburst of song.

> '*Wi' linked hands, we took the sands*
> *A-down yon winding river;*
> *And, oh! that hour and broomy bower,*
> *Can I forget it ever?*'

'How long can this go on?' Hazlitt groaned.

'Another hour should see us on the road,' reassured Campbell, deliberately misunderstanding. 'Just keep right on!'

If he starts singing again, Hazlitt promised himself, I'll kick him off the mountainside. I will. I really will.

But fortunately he was not put to the test as the path petered out in a shelf of smooth rock which required their full concentration to negotiate.

The Scotsman's timing was out by nearly thirty minutes but Hazlitt said nothing, feeling that his own short legs, plus the overhang of fatigue from his earlier adventures, had been the main cause.

'I didn't realise you were coming all the way,' he said to Campbell, who was now marching along at his shoulder on this broader path.

Now Campbell did burst into song, but as freedom was

in sight and there was no longer a mountainside to push him off, Hazlitt, inclined to clemency, grimaced and kept silent.

Soon their cleated boots were printing patterns in the heat-softened tarmac of the road. The early-evening sun was as warm as ever and Hazlitt felt in need of a rest, a cold shower and a long ice-packed drink. Only the first seemed immediately available, but for once in his life considerations other than personal comfort prevailed. He was uneasily aware of the hours that had elapsed since his flight from Coruisk and of the ease with which his escape route could be plotted.

'*Though you're tired and weary, still journey on . . .*' incanted Campbell and the advice sounded good. Even the singing was not so unpleasant to his ear now. There might be a great deal of comfort to be derived from having company along this lonely road.

There was other company besides, he suddenly realised, as a sound too discordant to be attributed even to Campbell mingled with his singing. A car engine somewhere behind them. He turned his head, in his present state of nervousness half expecting to see a 1927 bullet-proof Buick with tommy-gun protruding from the windows. The approaching vehicle was much more homely and reassuring. A battered and mud-spattered Ford Transit van whose amiably bucolic driver probably used it for bringing sheep down off the hills. It slowed down to their pace as it overtook them and the driver spoke to them through the open door, scratching his gingery hair in a kind of greeting.

'Grand day.'

'It is that,' responded Campbell.

'Are you tired with walking?'

'A touch,' grinned Campbell.

'I'm going as far as Sligachan. You're welcome to the ride.'

The driver halted the van without waiting for an answer. Hazlitt's weary legs took a couple of steps towards it, not needing any prompting from his mind; but to his surprise Campbell's hand gently engaged his arm and hindered further motion. The tall Scot spoke.

'I thank you, but no. Having stepped so far on our own two feet, we're jealous of our reputations. Drive safely.'

The driver shrugged, engaged the clutch and the van moved slowly by, but it stopped once more when it had completely overtaken them. For a moment Hazlitt thought it had broken down. Then the rear doors burst open and for the third time that day he found himself looking into the goldfish mouth of an automatic.

'You,' said its owner, a pale little man in a hot-looking blue serge suit. 'Inside.'

In fact he didn't say 'inside'. Hazlitt's mind provided the complete word, but the little man only had time for 'in' —or perhaps 'ins'—before Campbell (who could afford to be brave, screened as he was by his companion's body, Hazlitt commented later) brought his crummock whistling round in a short arc which ended at the gunman's left ear.

'Oh my God!' commented Hazlitt. The little man had seemed pale before, but now the blood perceptibly fled from his face as though a plug had been removed somewhere. His body hardly moved till Campbell pushed it roughly back into the van, catching the gun as it fell.

'Wait,' he commanded, quite unnecessarily, and ran round the side of the van. Seconds later he reappeared with the driver. For a music-hall Scotsman he seemed most efficient, Hazlitt thought.

'Inside,' said Campbell, managing the whole word. Hazlitt moved to obey.

'Not you,' said the Scot impatiently. *'You.'*

He poked the driver in the ribs. Silently the man

58

clambered aboard and began ministering to his partner.

'What are we going to do?' enquired Hazlitt, thinking suddenly and irrelevantly of a dish of aubergines stuffed with duck and pimentos he had once been served in Bordeaux. Perhaps it was a premonition that such things could never happen to him again. Or perhaps it was merely the colour of the contusion around the pale man's ear which had brought it to his mind.

'We can't leave them littering up the countryside,' said Campbell reasonably. 'I think on the whole it would be a goodly notion to remove them from the island. Aye. That's the thing. You drive, I'll sit in the back and keep them company.'

'But . . .' began Hazlitt. And stopped.

'What's the matter? Do you fancy sitting in the back, is that it?'

No, that wasn't it at all. Indeed, it was the very horror of that thought which had prevented Hazlitt from saying *but I can't drive*.

It was, in fact, not quite true. It had certainly been ten years since he had abandoned the motor-car as a means of transport. It had been shortly after he had given up smoking (except for the occasional Havana after a superb meal) on the grounds that it was a personal hazard and a public nuisance. The same arguments applied to the car, he had realised one wet Saturday lunchtime as he peered short-sightedly through a misty windscreen at the mad abacus of traffic on the motorway which lay between him and home. The police had been puzzled by his equable reaction when a few days later they tracked him down to report that his car had been found wheel-less and engine-less alongside the motorway approach road.

'That's all right,' he had said. 'I don't want it. Just leave it there till the rest goes.'

But driving was preferable to sitting with an aubergine-eared semi-corpse and his vengeful mate. Like riding a bike, it was something you never forgot, he assured himself as he climbed behind the wheel. But he remembered uneasily the perilous weeks which had followed his own return to cycling after giving up the car.

It took three attempts to get the thing started, another five to let the clutch in without stalling and a good ten minutes before he managed to negotiate the change from first to second gear. Behind him Campbell roared alternate abuse and advice, only ceasing when finally Hazlitt managed to reach third and thereafter ignored the gears and concentrated on keeping the vehicle moving along a relatively straight path at between twenty-five and thirty miles an hour. Only the small township of Broadford offered any significant obstacle to his progress and something desperately single-minded about the round face pressed almost flat against the windscreen persuaded even the most arrogant of motorists and suicidal of pedestrians to give way.

Then there was a nice straight stretch of road almost all the way to Kyleakin. Slowly his speed crept up as his mind felt confident enough to turn to thoughts other than keeping the van on the road.

'What am I doing?' he asked aloud. 'What the hell am I doing?'

It was a good question. Unlicensed, uninsured, he was driving along in a stolen van, kidnapping two men (one of whom was perhaps seriously injured, and both of whom he suspected desired seriously to injure *him*), aided and abetted in this by a Burns-quoting Scot whose own motives and role were, to say the least, shadowy.

But Hazlitt was not a rising star in the world of university administration for nothing. Two qualities were needed, perhaps dependent on each other—a grasp of essentials and a capacity for survival. Campbell's suggestion had been right, in part at least. It would be a good thing for Hazlitt to get off the island. Skye suddenly felt very small, a simple circle of rock and sand, a bull-ring into which ferocious beasts were being released by the minute.

But whether it would be a good thing to get off the island in present company he very much doubted. He began to examine his resources of ingenuity for means of freeing himself from these unwanted companions, but found he had used it all up for today. Yet he did not give up hope. In his job he had found that if only you approached an apparently insoluble problem at a fair turn of speed, it frequently went away. Speed was the thing.

A car horn blew abusively. A group of old ladies crossing the road skipped athletically out of the way, with balletic gestures whose meanings were beyond interpretation.

Hazlitt glanced at the dashboard and realised with horror that his metaphor of speed had become reality. Without noticing, he was roaring through the middle of Kyleakin at sixty-five miles an hour. The road turned sharply left into a one-way system on the approach to the ferry, but there was no chance of following. Instead the van went straight on past the 'no entry' signs, slowing reluctantly to the full pressure of Hazlitt's foot on the brake pedal. And suddenly, and having much the same effect as the Pacific had on stout Cortes, there before him stretched the sea.

The road became a causeway and ran down a gentle slope to the car-ferry landing, from which a packed boat was on the point of departing. There was obviously no chance of getting the van on it without causing a great deal of distress and damage to the vehicles and passengers already aboard, though this must have appeared Hazlitt's purpose as the reluctantly slowing van careered down the causeway. But he rose to the occasion, literally, standing hard on the brake and at the same time heaving the handbrake upwards as forcefully as possible. With dreadful high screeching noises, like a conventful of Viking-ravished nuns, the brakes locked and the van halted. Hazlitt was flung forward very painfully against the wheel. But he gauged from the noises in the rear that he had in fact come off best. Perhaps even better than best, he thought, sliding open the door, grabbing his rucksack and hopping out.

Irate and official-looking men in peaked caps were coming towards him down the causeway. He turned and ran towards the outgoing ferry. For a second he thought he was going to have to swim after it to the mainland, but only his feet got wet before helping hands aided him over the barrier and on to the deck.

'Thanks,' he gasped, 'thanks. Desperate hurry. Bad news at home. Mother ill. Ruined holiday.'

The madman suddenly became an object of sympathy. He turned away from the clucking noises which the Briton makes at such moments and looked back towards Skye. The locking of the brakes, it turned out, had merely been a temporary fusion, for they seemed to have released themselves now and the van was rolling slowly down the causeway into the sea. Out of the back tumbled two figures, neither of them kilted. The pale man with the aubergine ear had apparently made a good recovery. They pushed by the onlookers on the shore and disappeared towards the town. Hazlitt began to have serious doubts about the well-being of Campbell and memories of the two occasions on which the man had saved him from an unpleasant fate filled him with guilt.

But as the van plunged finally into the water, Campbell emerged, too late to avoid getting wet. His kilt spread out around him on the surface like a ballet dancer's skirt and he shouted with visible but inaudible fury after the departing boat.

'What's he say?' asked a man standing up through the sunshine roof of his car and busily clicking away with his camera. Hazlitt smiled up at him with great charm.

'He's an old sentimentalist,' he said. 'I think he may be singing *Will ye no come back again?*'

6

Caroline was packing. She opened her shoulder bag and to the British cheque book and cheque card it already contained she added her Diners' Club card, her American Express card and her Barclay card. After a little thought she further added her American cheque book, her Eurocard and her Thomas Cook's travellers cheques. And for good measure she chucked in her passport and her international driver's licence.

All told, in credit terms she reckoned she was good for about twenty thousand dollars.

In ready cash terms she had seven pounds and eighty-two pence.

She completed her packing by thrusting into the bag her toothbrush and as much underwear as it would hold. She recognised that her motives were neurotic as well as hygienic. She had been brought up to find it difficult to go anywhere without two or three suitcasefuls of unnecessary clothing. At 1 am, however, with stealth at a premium, she had no desire to encumber herself or make herself conspicuous by an excess of luggage. But though necessity demanded that she travel light, heredity required that her lightness should be as heavy as possible.

One last glance to make sure that her explanatory note

was clearly visible and she was on her way. She moved with exaggerated stealth and by the time she reached the pavement outside the garden gate she felt quite shattered by nervous exhaustion. But her spirits and her strength revived as she left the house behind and made her way to the nearest telephone box. A taxi to the station, a ticket, a train, and she would be away.

In her note she had said that the prospect of appearing in court was so distressing that she felt she had to get away, and proposed spending a few nights with a friend in London. She congratulated herself that she had struck the right note between distress and self-sufficiency. No one would set a search in motion on the grounds that she might be suicidal. On the other hand she knew too little of English law to gauge whether non-appearance in court would mean that the magistrate would issue a warrant for her arrest. She wished she could have consulted Thomas Poulson about this, but the early hours of the morning did not seem a good time to ask for free legal advice.

In any case her note would ensure that any search was centred on London, which was one place she had no intention of going. While the hunt was on in the great metropolis, she would be breathing the freer, fresher air of bonnie Scotland. She almost laughed aloud. All a good fugitive needed was the ability to trail a few nice and smelly red herrings. She stepped out of the phone box and waited for her taxi.

'You're sure she's going to Scotland?'

'Edinburgh is what she asked for,' said the flaxen-haired man.

'Oh Jesus. These bloody Americans. What's the time?'

'Just after two.'

'Oh Jesus. I'll never get back to sleep, you realise that?'

'Yes, sir. I'm sorry. Look, what do I do?'

'You'd better follow her, I suppose.'

'Follow?'

'That's your assignment, isn't it? Surveillance. Well, surveille away. Give me a ring when you can, preferably at a more civilised hour. Tell me what she's up to. Perhaps she just wants to visit the festival.'

'That's not till August.'

'You don't imagine she knows what month of the year it is, do you? Just keep her out of our hair, that's all I ask.'

'What about this shop-lifting case? Won't there be a warrant?'

'For God's sake, man! She's not due in court till to-morrow. And even then . . . no, not for that, but it might not be a bad idea if she looks like being a trouble. I'll fix something . . . but bed first. Have a nice trip. Good night.'

'Good night, sir.'

The phone was replaced.

'And get stuffed,' added the flaxen-haired man.

'And get stuffed,' added the Old Etonian.

Caroline had never been in Scotland before and made her way out of the gloom of Edinburgh's Waverley Station with all the eagerness of a New World seeker after the Old. She was not disappointed. A couple of minutes drifting with the morning work crowd brought her first sight of the castle. It was a soul-stirring sight, looming over the town with all the protectiveness and the threat of an Old Testament deity. But other needs took over and she crossed the road to the built-up side of Princes Street and after a bit of searching found a place which provided both breakfast and a ladies' room.

Porridge and Aberdeen kippers, she recalled Hazlitt saying, were the only dishes one could order with confidence anywhere north of Hadrian's Wall. With half

67

the rainfall and one decent restaurant, the country would be as near to Paradise as man could hope for here below, he had asserted.

She ate her porridge and kippers with relish, at the same time recognising the restrictiveness of such a diet. She also recognised in herself a reluctance to settle down and work out her next move. The source of this reluctance was obvious—lack of data. She knew, or believed she knew, that Hazlitt was in Scotland. It seemed likely he was in trouble. It seemed likely that *his* being in trouble had something to do with *her* being in trouble. Therefore for both their sakes it seemed a good thing to seek him out and exchange notes. Which was why she was presently sitting in an Edinburgh café drinking vile black coffee (the alternative had been offered as 'brown' ... What did they add? Mud?).

The only clue to his precise whereabouts was a memory of places he had mentioned in conversation with her. That he would have headed for somewhere familiar rather than braved new terrain seemed a fair deduction. Which left her with a list of half a dozen 'possibles' (plus the other possibility that he had gone somewhere he hadn't mentioned). But which to start at and what to do once she got there, she had no idea.

What I need, she thought, is a clue. Everyone deserves at least one clue in this life. It's time I got mine.

She realised she was being a little unfair to whoever provided clues as she had already received one or two fair pointers back in Lincoln. But yesterday's gratitude was as cold as yesterday's porridge. Clues should come daily like newspapers.

A man sat at the table opposite her glanced at her with disconcerting lack of interest and raised his newspaper in front of his face.

It was the Scottish edition of one of the popular dailies and Caroline looked across at it without interest until suddenly, violently, it struck her that this was more than a newspaper, this was her clue!

There on the front page was a picture. It seemed to show a van half submerged in water, with a bearded ballerina rising from, or sinking below, the waves. But this unusual scene was not what caught Caroline's eye. In the foreground, near enough the camera to be out of focus, was part of a man's head. Fuzzy it was and ill-defined, but at this distance it seemed to Caroline to have the unmistakable form and contours of William Blake Hazlitt's.

She stood up and went nearer. Fuzziness increased and it might have been a turnip. Back two paces, however, and there it was again. Hazlitt's balding dome, distinctive as Edinburgh Castle.

The man lowered his paper as she advanced again and looked at her with the wary puzzlement of one who fears he is being threatened by eccentricity.

'I'm sorry,' said Caroline. 'Your paper.'

Perhaps her accent made the man think he was being accused of some illicit paternity. Whatever the case he rose and shook his head, holding out the newspaper before him like a charm to ward off evil spirits.

'Thanks,' said Caroline, taking it and examining the picture eagerly.

Over the sea to Skye? said the caption whimsically. There followed a light-hearted and very sketchy account of how the van had rolled into the water in the wake of the ferry. But this Caroline disregarded. There was no reason for her to connect the amphibious van with Hazlitt's presence on the ferry. All it meant was that her immediate problem was solved.

'Thanks,' she said again, but the owner of the paper had disappeared. Shrugging her shoulders, she carefully tore out the front page, folded it and thrust it into her already overcrowded bag.

69

'Can I have my check please?' she said to the waitress, who had been watching the scene with lively interest. 'And tell me. How do I get to the Island of Skye?'

'Lost him!' exclaimed the Old Etonian. 'That's very careless of you. Very careless. No, no excuses, please. One of you had better take a chance and head north. Yes, that would be best. The other can cast around a bit, try to pick up a scent. Or he may have learned low cunning from the natives and try to double back. If he heads south, we'll spot him, never fear. Some of us are still earning our money.'

He replaced the receiver and went back to bed.

'Lost him!' exclaimed the young man. 'And Sangster dead. For Christ's sake, there's only one of him, isn't there? And he's getting old and fat. You go and get him bloody quick. Make it look good if you can, but, above all, *get him.*'

He slammed down the phone in anger. A capacity for decision-making drew notice, that was certain. But it only drew approval if it were matched by an equal capacity for acting on those decisions.

'What is it this time?' demanded the Old Etonian. 'Durban? I might have known. You've lost her? What's happening to everybody today? No, no, don't say anything, be it apology or impudence. Just find her, that's all. Oh, the horror of it all!'

Hazlitt sat in the back of a mini-bus, allowing his lips to move in some kind of synchronism with the jolly protest song the six geology students from Manchester were belting out with much gusto. His flight from Kyle of Lochalsh, the mainland arrival point of the Skye ferry,

70

had taken him as far as Garve in mid Cromarty on a public transport bus. The dangers of this mode of travel were obvious. It left a trail easy to follow. Drivers and conductors could easily be prodded to recall such a figure as he was. It was because of this fear that he had descended near Garve where the road divided, going south-east to Dingwall or Inverness, or north-west to Ullapool. He had spent an uncomfortable mosquito-bitten night on the banks of a river and found himself longing for a soft bed and crisp fresh sheets. But the following morning brought him a stroke of fortune when he ran into the geologists who were camping a little farther upstream. They were a sociable crew and it had been easy to solicit an invitation to join them in their mini-bus. Their ultimate destination was Durness on the north coast of Sutherland, whose rocks seemed to have some peculiar attraction for students of the earth. The main attraction for Hazlitt was that with a bit of luck his tracks would fade out completely at this point. If he kept himself inconspicuous between here and Durness there would be no way of picking up his scent again.

Though, of course, he had thought that on Skye.

He wondered if once more he would be able to create that simple, timeless Tom and Jerry world which he had inhabited by Coruisk. He doubted it. It had not been just the mosquitoes which had thwarted his attempts to sleep last night. The past and the future were pressing in hard on him and there had been times in the night when there had seemed only one possible escape from both. Devils, he recalled, had appeared to Faustus, offering knives and ropes to entice him to dispatch himself. The thought made him shudder. But had some benevolent old devil, made up like a *maître-d'hôtel*, appeared in the night and offered him some gentle, taste-less opiate gently stirred into a glass of Armagnac (not cognac—the dillution of an Armagnac he felt he might

71

just bear, but not a cognac), then he might have fallen. But his mind had started working back over possible menus for this his last meal—a *soufflé à la liqueur* perhaps, with a *Château d'Yquem*; preceded by *Rognons de Veau Flambes* with a bottle of Burgundy. *Clos de Tart*? Too rich a combination? Then why not? . . . and so on. And only the mosquitoes had come, and then morning, and here he was still running to some quite unattainable refuge where the croissants were fresh and the brandies very very old.

'You all right?' asked Eric, the leader of the party.

Hazlitt realised the singing had stopped but that his mouth was still open and shutting in silent harmony.

'Oh yes. Fine thanks. I was miles away. Where are we?'

'Soon be at Kylesku. There's a pub there.' He glanced at his watch. 'Just in time for opening. We'll have a pint and a sandwich, then go over the ferry.'

Another ferry. The sea came at you from all sides in this country. He glanced back out of the rear window. Nothing. Dare he start feeling safe for a while? It would be foolish, certainly. But he was not built for perpetual trepidation.

He moistened his lips and grinned at Eric.

'That'll be nice,' he said.

It was nice. After his second pint of heavy he began to feel all was right with the world. Perhaps everything was a simple misunderstanding, easily cleared up by a rational and tolerant approach from both sides. Correction. All three sides. How nice it would be to return to the *status quo*, looking forward to Africa with beyond that the prospect of Stewart Stuart's retirement to keep the digestive juices running. A watercress soup of a life, simple, creamy and refreshing, the only fly in it being the prospect of separation from Caroline for a few months.

Caroline. He shuddered to think how close he had

come to making a serious committal in that direction only a few weeks earlier. To have done so, to have come out in the open, might, of course, have brought rejection, even derision. He hoped not. But had his declaration been accepted, reciprocated, then the thought of the worry and unease he would now be causing the girl would have been intolerable. As it was she might be a little piqued, perhaps even slightly hurt, by his sudden most unchivalrous disappearance, but that was all. She'd get over it; their relationship would become a mere episode, a brush with middle-aged, English academic eccentricity. There had been plenty of young eligibles in the wings waiting to take over when he found the pace too hot. Tarquin and Sholto, those well-bred young shits in his own office, for instance. Or Tom Poulson, that vague lawyer even. Not to mention the whole horrid hairy and horny student brigade.

Oh yes, he thought gloomily (going up to the bar for another pint and thus not noticing the large white shooting-brake containing two men, one with a thick ear, and an exasperated-looking woman, which drove straight on to the ferry), oh yes, he thought, she'll have lost sight of me by now. Wherever she is at this moment, she'll be all right.

Caroline was driving hard through Glen Coe determined to perpetrate a second and more fearful massacre on any sheep, cyclists or caravans that got in her way. It had been a frustrating morning. The car-hire firms she had visited in Edinburgh had all with one accord assured her that hire cars were at this moment rarer in Scotland than good cooks. Finally she had descended upon a used-car lot, picked out the first post-1970 car she saw with a current road-fund licence and offered to buy it. The 'salesman', an elderly Scot, whose attention to her needs was continually interrupted by calls for his services at the petrol pumps, advised her that his 'laddie' looked after that part of the business and would be back in 'no time at a'.'

Finally Caroline wrote a cheque for the amount asked and thrust it at him, along with her full array of cheque and credit cards. The old man turned them over hesitantly, his eyes more concerned with the display of panties which had spilt out of the bag.

'What's the problem?' demanded Caroline. 'Do I get the car or don't I?'

'Well noo,' said the old man, turning the cheque over and over in his hands. 'Do you no' have proof of your identity?'

'Such as? Such as?' cried Caroline.

'Well, say, an old envelope with your address on?'

'Would a postcard do?'

'Aye. Aye, I reckon so.'

'Wait,' she said. 'Just you wait. Don't go away.'

She gathered up her things, went into a newsagent's shop next door to the garage and bought a view of the Forth Bridge. Quickly she addressed it to herself.

'Here,' she said to the old man. 'Will that do?'

Two minutes later she was in the car and on her way.

There was no straight road to Skye, she discovered, merely a choice of circumgyrations. To complicate matters the roads were narrow, seemingly packed with cyclists, completely open to suicidal sheep, and bestridden by monstrous, dangerously swaying caravans.

'No man is worth this,' she told herself, cutting in on one travelling suburban bungalow in order to avoid collision with another. Both drivers blew their horns abusively, but Caroline ignored them. She had grown exhausted with making rude gestures a good hour earlier. 'But,' she went on to herself, 'if any man *is* worth it, then he's *really* worth it!'

She nodded vigorously and pressed her foot hard on the

accelerator with the certainty of a logician who has produced a flawless syllogism.

Hazlitt would have recognised and approved of the logical system thus demonstrated. He himself had just carried out a similar feat of disjunctive reasoning, to wit, that it is better to be driven by a man made capable by drink than by a man made incapable by it.

Eric had indicated that he and Lawrence, the only two qualified drivers in the party, had embraced the dangerous Scottish habit of taking a whisky chaser with their beer. The result was a certain dissociation of sensibility which made driving difficult. Either they rested at Kylesku for another couple of hours to sober up, or perhaps Hazlitt could help . . . ?

After his recent experiences in the van, Hazlitt had felt certain he would never be able to sit behind a wheel again. But three pints of the 'heavy', plus a desire to keep moving, made him agree without demur.

He moved the mini-bus into position for the ferry. It was a short crossing here over Loch Glendhu and the ferry was small, taking only half a dozen cars at a time. As they waited for the south-bound cars to disembark, Hazlitt saw in his mirror a small convoy come into line behind him, headed by that scourge of Highland driving, a caravan. A couple of cars behind this was a red Capri, whose driver now got out and glared contemptuously at the caravanners.

Hazlitt stared into the mirror in disbelief, then stuck his head out of the window and peered back to make sure.

It was Tom. Not (thank heaven!) Tom (Mark II), last seen lying dead by the waters of Coruisk, but Tom (Mark I), the burly, sinister figure in the fawn raincoat and brown trilby, who had first aroused Hazlitt's fears yesterday (could it only be yesterday?) morning.

75

Coincidence? Possibly. There was nothing except that initial intuitive fear to connect this man with any of his pursuers. And the North of Scotland offered such a comparatively limited selection of roads that it was not surprising to re-encounter other travellers.

The ferry was empty now. Tom turned back to his car, but as he did so, their eyes met.

There was not a flicker of expression, not a hint of emotion, but Hazlitt knew with the certainty of a seventh child of a seventh child that he had been recognised.

It seemed possible for a happy moment that the caravan would take up so much room that the Capri would be left behind. But it just made it and when they reached the other side the Capri even made an effort to disembark before the caravan. Hazlitt was delighted to see the attempt thwarted as he pulled away up the hill from the ferry. It gave him a chance to get some kind of lead and he urged the mini-bus forward with all the rusty skill at his command.

It was not a road for fast driving. It was a wild road, narrow, winding, dangerous, at one with the turbulent landscape which it traversed. Sudden views of lochs and bays flashed on the eye between grassy knolls and outbursts of massive rock. It was as if the landscape had boiled up and suddenly set. From time to time there were small lay-bys which acted as passing points. It provided a stern test of judgment and often a clash of wills when two cars approached each other. For Hazlitt, desperately trying to make the best speed he could in his unwieldy and unfamiliar vehicle, it was nightmarish. Fortunately the geologists were still sufficiently euphoric or somnolent from their protracted halt at the inn for his excesses to go unremarked.

The road behind remained clear, though there was never much of it visible at any one time. His spirits began to raise themselves slightly. Perhaps he could get to Durness without being overtaken. Perhaps he could go to earth there and sort things out in his mind.

Perhaps Tom (Mark I) was, after all, merely a chance tourist, seeking the solace of nature after fifty weeks in a stuffy office.

Perhaps . . . there was a flash of red on the road behind him, then he was round another bend and it was gone. Perhaps it had never been. Oh no. That way disaster lies. Admit what you see. A sixty-yard straight. Foot down and get the needle up to fifty. Jesus how these things bucked and swayed!

'What's the rush, squire?' asked Eric. 'We'll be there for opening, so take it easy.'

He slowed for the bend. Behind him, at the other end of the straight, appeared the Capri. That was it. He might as well slow down to a crawl.

But he was finding out quite a lot about the psychology of the hunted, especially the hunted who had been shot at and half drowned and who had three pints of the 'heavy' in his belly. This creature didn't slow down until exhaustion brought it down. And even then, perhaps, it turned at bay and fought. But he wouldn't know that till the moment came.

He took the bend on two wheels and immediately thrust down on the accelerator once more. Everyone was awake now, surprised to find themselves all at the same side of the bus with most of their luggage.

'For Christ's sake, watch it!'

'Stop the bus, I want a pee.'

'I think I'm going to be sick.'

'*Please!*'

'Oh Jesus Mary Mother of . . .'

Coming towards them was a truck, just a medium-sized truck, but on this road and at this moment it assumed the dimensions of a Juggernaut. There was a

77

passing spot just ahead, but it would have been impossible to halt in it even had Hazlitt so desired. He kept his foot down and concentrated his attention on the next passing spot about seventy yards on. The truck had almost reached it and the driver was flashing his headlights madly, whether in anger or some kind of signal Hazlitt did not know.

The red Capri was closing fast. The truck had not quite reached the lay-by when the mini-bus passed it. The nearside wheels strayed off the road on to a narrow strip of rock-lined grass. One of the hub caps hit a rock, scraped along it with a terrifying screech, then they were past and back on tarmac again.

The geologists were silent now with the silence of utter fear. Hazlitt felt it emanating from them.

'I'm sorry,' he said. 'I'm sorry.'

But his apology was of little use. He swung round the next bend and saw why the truck-driver had been flashing his lights. Parked by the roadside was a large white shooting-brake, jacked up and with one wheel removed. There was just enough room to squeeze by for a driver of care and skill, travelling at five or six miles an hour.

Hazlitt's speed was eight times that and in any case his attention was very much distracted from the task.

The man changing the wheel was the aubergine-eared gunman. The ginger man standing beside him was his driver companion. And the woman sitting on a rock by the roadside, smoking a cigarette, was Tom (Mark II)'s companion from Coruisk.

He found he had braked hard. The mini-bus skidded elegantly, the two men leapt aside with athletic grace, even the sound of the collison had something almost harmonious about it.

'I'm sorry,' repeated Hazlitt as the echoes died away. None of the geologists seemed injured but all looked badly shaken. He felt guilty at the ill repayment he had given them for their kindness. Outside, the trio from the shooting-brake were regrouping. The least he could do for his companions was spare them any involvement in gun play. He slid open the door and stepped out, hands slightly raised in surrender. Aubergine-ear had his right hand resting menacingly in his jacket pocket.

'Please,' said Hazlitt, shaking his head. *'Whither thou goest I will go, thy people shall be . . .'*

But he didn't finish. There was another screeching and wailing of brakes behind him and round the bend came the red Capri.

Hazlitt flung himself out of its path and tumbled down a rocky incline into a saucer of boggy turf. Above, Tom (Mark I) proved himself a very superior kind of driver by successfully evading the mini-bus. Indeed he would probably have evaded everything had it not been for the presence on the road of the Skye trio. Unable to believe such a thing could happen twice, their evasion tactics were much more laboured than before, and Tom (Mark I), faced with a choice of running them down, or proceeding off the road into a natural car trap of rock and bog, or side-swiping the white shooting-brake, opted for the last.

After the noise there was a long silence. Nobody seemed very interested in stirring. The geologists made no move to leave their bus, Tom (Mark I) sat quietly and impassively in his car, the Skye trio seemed bent on impressing a permanent outline of themselves into the ground.

Hazlitt rose and checked himself for damage. All appeared well.

There are times, he thought, when a man of breeding does not speak but slips away with unobtrusive speed. Such a time was now.

He began to move with tasteful discretion away from the road and quickly disappeared among the rocky contours of the countryside.

7

The geography of Great Britain had occupied no great part of Caroline's education. She knew from its appearance on her nursery globe how small it was compared with the great landmass of the Americas, or continental Europe, or Asia. And though she had outgrown her childish belief that her father's homeland was a kind of Lilliput from which he on account of his unusual size had been expelled, she still retained an unspoken sense of miniaturism about the place.

Even the journey from Edinburgh to Skye through some of the most splendid scenery she had met with did not dispel this. It was a long journey, true, but it was the insane bloody roads that made it so. A six-lane freeway would have made it a pre-breakfast jaunt.

Thus it came as a nasty surprise to her to realise that Skye (not even a real island, she had been told, but a mere *isle*) was rather more than a couple of acres in size and had an interior and a population large enough to swallow Hazlitt without trace.

She was back to her California private-eye role. This time she did have a photograph to slap down on bar counters, but unfortunately this photograph was worse than no photograph at all. She tried it out in Kyleakin, persuading a half-distrustful, half-amused barman to retreat to the optimum distance of eight feet and try to identify the vague outline of Hazlitt's head. The two or three occupants of the bar (which was in an hotel and labelled, with true Scots economy, 'public bar' on the street entrance and 'cocktail lounge' on the hotel entrance) joined in the game. One of them affected to recognise the Prime Minister in the blurred arrangement of grey dots; another averred it was a thumbprint on the negative. Only a large bearded man in a tweed suit seemed truly interested and asked her many questions about Hazlitt's appearance. His own face seemed vaguely familiar, but as she found most bearded men practically indistinguishable she was not much occupied by this.

His efforts to help were interrupted by a summons to the telephone, upon which Caroline attempted to use the bar for its official purpose only to find it had closed. However, as a consolation, the barman offered two pieces of advice.

'If your mannie's a camping and hiking sort of fellow, you'd best ask after him in Sligachan or some such place. He'd no' spend much time about here.'

This made sense, but his second suggestion—to enquire of the men who worked on the ferry—made even more. Caroline realised guiltily that she had driven aboard, sat plunged in thought in her car during the brief crossing, and disembarked on Skye, without once considering the human agencies involved. She had once mocked Hazlitt with a charge of affectation when he had sent his compliments to a corner-café chef who had produced an unusually tasty lamb chop on a cheap businessman's lunch menu.

'You think it's all done by machines, my dear,' he had reprimanded her. 'There's a craftsman in that kitchen. He deserves our praise.'

Now she set off down to the harbour feeling positively apologetic. Outside the hotel she was overtaken by the bearded Scot on his way to the car park.

'Good luck,' he said to her. *'Thine be ilka joy and treasure, Peace, enjoyment, love, and pleasure.'*

'Thanks,' she answered, feeling disproportionately cheered by this gratuitous encouragement.

It was hard to interview the men on the ferry and her sense of apology rapidly disappeared. They spent their lives in perpetual motion. When the ship stopped they moved; only when the vessel was in motion was there a chance of getting hold of one of them, so Caroline travelled across to the mainland and back with the ferry.

She no longer bothered with the newspaper clipping, which had proved pretty useless as a visual aid so far, but offered instead a graphic description of Hazlitt to anyone who would listen.

At the fith time of asking she struck oil.

'Aye,' said a young rather oil-stained boathand. 'The wee man wi' the van, ye mean? I mind him fine. That was a laugh, eh? Excuse me.'

The ferry was docking at the other side and he set about his business of organising the influx of cars, leaving Caroline impatiently awaiting his return.

'What do you mean, with the van?' she asked, as they began juddering their way over the sea to Skye once more.

'Is it no' him ye mean?' asked the youth. 'Funny wee fellow, very red in the face, thin in the hair and stickit-out ears? Och, I'm sorry, it's no' yer fether, is it?'

'No,' said Caroline with a grin, storing the conversation up for later use. 'But the van. You don't mean the van in the water?'

There had been no reason hitherto to think of any direct connection between Hazlitt and the central incident of the photograph. It had merely seemed a happy coincidence that he should have been a spectator and got his picture in the paper. But now . . .

Quickly she produced the newspaper cutting and showed it to her informant.

'That's it,' he said. 'He hoppit out of it like a scalded cat, he was sae keen to catch the ferry. Well, he managed it, but the brake canna ha' been properly locked, for the van came rolling doon the causeway after him. Mon, it was funny!'

He laughed delightedly at the memory, but Caroline did not join in. Staring at the picture, she felt her heart sink as another 'obvious' fact she had completely missed now shouted out at her. The blurb underneath only referred to 'the Skye ferry' and she had foolishly assumed that this meant the ferry Hazlitt was on was making the crossing *to* Skye. Instead it was now clear as she glanced up and looked at the fast-approaching harbour of Kyleakin that the boat in the picture was leaving the island.

Which meant that the formidable task of tracking him down on Skye was now dwarfed by the impossible prospect of seeking him almost anywhere on the mainland.

'Shit,' she said, and wondered again if it was worth it.

Despondent, she left the ferry and walked slowly back into Kyleakin along the line of cars waiting to embark. Halfway along the queue, she passed a battered cream-and-brown Peugeot. In it, listening to the radio, was the bearded Scot. He didn't notice her, but she noticed him.

Convinced that she was merely over-compensating for her previous stupidity and clutching at straws, Caroline stepped into an open shop doorway and dug out her newspaper clipping once more.

If Hazlitt had come out of that van, then he had something to do with anyone else who had been in it. And the more she stared from the bearded face in the paper to the bearded face in the car, the more she became convinced they were one and the same.

It was crazy, but what the hell! It was pointless staying on Skye for anything but a holiday and a holiday was not what she felt like just now.

She set off at a brisk, athletic jog-trot to where she had parked her car.

The flaxen-haired man who had driven off the ferry behind her slowly followed.

'Yes, sir. I know she went to Skye. I caught up with her there.'

'Clever boy. What's she doing there?'

'She's not there any longer, sir. She left as soon as I arrived.'

'Discerning girl. Heading for home, I hope?'

'No, sir. North.'

'Oh no!'

'Is that bad, sir?'

'Tell me, Durban, how is it that this transatlantic trollop so rapidly picks up trails it takes my own highly trained men ages to uncover?'

'You mean Hazlitt's up there too?'

'Yes. Continuing his highly successful evasive tactics. Happily, he is making the other lot look as foolish as ourselves. Where are you now?'

'Ullapool.'

'Such odd places. Wait. Yes, yes, it must exist; it appears in my old school atlas. What's happening?'

'Her car seems to have blown up. I can see her out of the phone-box window. She's talking with a mechanic. She seems to be having some difficulty with the language.'

'It would be nice if she were stranded.'

'I'll do my best, sir. But it's going to take a lot to strand this one. She's a pretty determined girl.'

'Please, Durban, no sentimental admiration. For all our sakes, she must be prevented from meddling further. There's the shop-lifting thing, of course, but that's all very vague. Look, leave it with me, will you? Don't lose her and by tomorrow morning I'll fix it so that she can be taken right out. These damned Americans. After a while they begin to believe their own movies.'

The University Staff Club bar was unusually full for so early in the evening. Sir Walter Tyas had put in one of his rare appearances, his silky grey hair, three inches longer than when he was in politics, creating an aesthetic contrast with Stewart Stuart's grizzled stubble as their two heads almost met over their drinks.

'There's Nevis now,' said Stuart, looking towards the bar.

'Ah, James!' called Sir Walter. 'Come and join us. How are you? Another drink?'

'Later, perhaps.'

'James, we were just talking about the new research grant for your department. Your efforts have really put us on the map, you know. There's lots of money available. Lots. Congratulations.'

'Thanks.'

'You realise, of course, the ministry will want to be sure about . . . Well, you know, the kind of thing that's going on. Who's doing what. And who knows about it. You know what ministries are.'

'I have my suspicions,' said Nevis.

'Perhaps you could drop in at my office some time and we'll have a talk. Yes, we'll have a talk when you drop in,' said Stuart.

'That will be nice,' said Nevis. 'Is Bill Hazlitt back yet?'

The Vice-Chancellor and Registrar exchanged glances.

'No,' said Stuart. 'No. He's not. He's not back. Anything I can do?'

'Oh no. Nothing official. I was just enquiring.'

'Sorry to interrupt,' said Tarquin Adams' elegant voice, 'but there's a phone call for you, Professor Nevis. Someone called Servis, I think. Sounded a bit grim, I'm afraid. Servis without a smile.'

He got none here either. Nevis excused himself and left, passing Thomas Poulson and Sholto Greig in deep conversation at the bar. Tarquin watched him go, willed the Vice-Chancellor to invite him to sit down, failed, and began looking round to see if he could spot the Reader in Moral Philosophy. It was a nice warm evening, just right for a swim.

'You realise,' said the mechanic, 'it's a disaster?'

'But it's only got thirty thousand on the clock!'

'Aye. The second time round, perhaps. They shouldna hire out sic things.'

'I didn't hire it,' said Caroline. 'I bought it.'

'You don't say? Well, well,' said the mechanic, shaking his head in what looked more like admiration than disapproval of such a feat of salesmanship.

'How long will it take?'

'Pardon?'

'How long, oh lord, how long?' moaned Caroline. 'Look, you fixum magic waggon without horse, how many moons?'

'I might have it ready by the morn,' said the mechanic.

'Tomorrow!'

'Aye. On the other hand, I canna promise. Sometimes medicine man speak with forked tongue too.'

'Gee, thanks,' said Caroline, raising a grin. But she

felt far from happy as she gazed out past the little white township up the rising road along which the Peugeot had disappeared to heaven knew what destination.

Hazlitt had dined well. His chosen path had led him parallel to the road for a couple of miles to a small village boasting a petrol pump, an hotel and a café. A police car went through it as he approached and he felt certain it must be going to investigate the accident he had left behind him. He peered into the café which seemed to be full of small children eating mince and tatties. A notice in the window assured him that no deep frying took place on Sundays. A religious precaution, he felt sure. Ye who deep fry on the Sabbath shall yourselves be deep fried.

His own supplies were running very low and he thought for a moment of stopping for a meal. *Coquilles St Jacques à la Provençale* might have proved irresistible, but it wasn't worth taking such a risk for mince and tatties.

As he walked by the hotel, he saw through the open front door a table on which it seemed returning fishermen deposited their catch. Someone had had a good day. Two fine salmon and half a dozen sea trout of various sizes. For fishing as a sport he had a great contempt. Killing things for pleasure had no appeal, but for food was a different matter entirely. Without compunction, he stepped through the door, selected two small sea trout, wrapped them in a copy of the *Scotsman* which someone had conveniently left on the reception desk, and retreated in good order.

He baked them whole in a turf oven of his own design, sitting on a high rocky peninsula which fell away in near-vertical slices on either side, like a cut loaf falling forward into the sea. In the mouth of each fish he placed one of the ready-made *bouquets garnis* he carried with him and

88

he washed each delicately flavoured mouthful down with a nip of the Highland Park 100 proof straight malt he felt no well-equipped walker should be without.

The sea was calm, no wind stirred, but still the weight of the vast Atlantic swinging in the cradle of the moon was enough to fill his sleep with the growling of waters as they gnawed and sucked at the dark bones of the land.

8

Caroline's life at the moment was full of geophysical surprises. In his bitterer moments her father had assured her it was always pouring down in Britain and especially in Scotland. Now she was finding that the farther north she got, the hotter the weather became.

The Ullapool medicine man had not, after all, spoken with forked tongue and she would have got away before nine o'clock had not some joker slashed all her tyres during the night. The garage owner was most distressed and immediately rang the police, a course of action which filled Caroline with some concern. She was suddenly conscious that she should have attended court the previous day and though she assured herself that Professor Nevis would be able to cover up for her in some way, meeting the police did not feel like a good idea.

In addition she was aware that the phrase 'some joker' was euphemistically dismissive. She had begun to distrust accident. Anything that happened at the moment was likely to have a purpose. So she urged the mechanic to greater speed, herself assisted as best she could, and was able to get into the newly tyred car and drive away before the investigatory forces arrived.

'I have to be in Inverness this afternoon,' she assured the garage proprietor. 'If I'm needed I can be reached at the Station Hotel. Okay?'

She felt quite proud of the lie as she drove due north.

Now it was early afternoon and she was driving with all windows open, wondering why the British never thought of putting air conditioning in their cars. At least in the small township of Durness, which she was now entering, they seemed to have had the sense to adopt the southern custom of siesta. There was scarcely a soul in sight, all the buildings seemed to be shut up and deserted, even the cars which were parked in some profusion gave an impression of being abandoned.

She began to be worried. Above all things at the moment she wanted a long cold drink and this place held out little promise of providing one. Perhaps the Vikings had landed or the plague had struck.

When she enquired of an old man with a stick where everyone was and he muttered something about a gathering, her facetious guess about the plague suddenly became a possibility.

'Gathering? You mean like a boil?' she enquired, stepping back a little.

'The Games, lassie,' he replied contemptuously. 'The Games.'

The truth became evident round the next bend. Distantly on a grassy headland overlooking the sea, the good people of Durness and at least an equal number of visitors had indeed gathered. Pipe music came drifting mournfully towards her and what looked like an animated telegraph pole momentarily reared its length into the breathless air.

It came to Caroline that probably her only chance of getting a long cool drink in this place today would be at the Gathering.

With a sigh she parked her car and set off across the field in search of a refreshment tent. It was not difficult to find. Only the pipe band could have hoped to compete with the happy chatter that was coming from its vicinity

92

and as most of the pipers themselves seemed now to have abandoned the charms of music and joined the drinkers, it was no contest.

What most of those near the bar seemed to be doing, Caroline rapidly observed, was getting as much whisky as possible into their bellies via a kind of bucket chain of cardboard cups. Whether they were motivated by some fear that the cardboard would absorb the liquid or, worse, grow soggy and spill it, Caroline could not say. But she began to suspect that her own desired concoction was going to be difficult to find. Nevertheless she asked for it. Hazlitt, who made much more fuss about food and drink than she ever did, would have found her ridiculous. 'Good catering,' he said, 'is doing what is possible perfectly. Only half-wits and Americans always expect the impossible and never appreciate perfection.' To which Caroline had offered the only possible counter: 'Oh wrap up, you pompous gnome.' This moment had been if not a turning point, at least the first screech of a rusty hinge in their relationship.

'I should like,' she said, to the amiably smiling girl at the other side of the bar, 'a dry Cinzano with ice, lime juice, a sprig of bruised mint if you've got it, but otherwise a zest of lemon will do, all topped up with soda.'

To her surprise the girl nodded brightly, seized a cardboard cup, thrust it over the counter and said, 'Fifteen pee.'

It contained, of course, whisky. Caroline shook her head. Her principles demanded that she start all over again with her explanation, but the flesh was suddenly weak and wilting.

She turned, left the tent, bought herself a huge ice-cream cone and settled down to watch the Games.

They seemed an interesting mixture of the usual athletic pastimes and the peculiarly Scottish ones of hurling weights and telegraph poles (called 'cabers', with a short 'a') great distances and heights. Caroline could not really claim it grabbed her. Athletic pursuits of any kind usually bored her. Though there was, she had to admit, a certain kinky pleasure to be got out of watching scenes like that before her now, in which a kilted man swung a huge metal weight between his legs, then hurled the thing high over his head and ran quickly forward before it could descend on him. She presumed the first person to incur a serious injury in the groin or the skull lost.

The sporting world was, she realised, another area of complete lack of harmony with Hazlitt. Truthfully speaking, she thought we have nothing in common. Why do I bother?

For a moment, standing there almost as far north as she could get, eating an ice-cream she hadn't wanted, watching a spectacle she didn't care for, surrounded by people she didn't know, it seemed a very good question.

Then she saw Hazlitt and her heart turned over. It was like being struck in the stomach by a blunt instrument. In fact, looking down, she realised that if a Great Dane's head could be called a blunt instrument this is just what had happened. Dogs provided another area of disagreement with Hazlitt, who had now disappeared from view. She cared little for most dogs. Big dogs that seemed intent on ravishing her, she hated. The brute reared up and attempted to place its paws on her shoulders. Over its great slobbering head she saw Hazlitt again. He was on the far side of the ground, separated from her by a mere fifty yards of grass and, of course, half a hundredweight of canine flesh.

A shirt-sleeved, handkerchief-hatted man carrying a thonged leather dog lead and wearing on his face the revolting smile of one who thinks attention from his pet is like a mention in the New Year's Honours List, nodded encouragingly at Caroline and said, 'It's your ice-cream he's after, lassie. Och aye, he's a rare boy for the ice-cream.'

'You don't say? Then he can bloody well have it!' exclaimed Caroline, and thrust the remnants of her cone into the animal's mouth. Far from being gratified at such largesse, the animal began to howl piteously and retreated behind the legs of its owner, whose reaction was equally lacking in pleasure.

'Hey now, hey now, there there, hen, it's a'richt, hey now, what for did ye do that? This is a highly strung beastie . . .'

But Caroline had not time to argue or to utter even a small selection of the twenty or thirty pieces of fine abuse which came to her mind. She had lost Hazlitt again and began ranging around trying to catch a glimpse of that familiar sun-reddened pate.

There he was! Someone had stopped him. A woman. Caroline's heart turned over again, this time for a different cause. Could the answer to all the mysteries be simply this, that he wanted to get away with some female whose identity needed to be kept secret? A colleague's wife perhaps? Or the Vice-Chancellor's daughter. Or even that awful girl in the Registry who came to work mini-skirted, obscenely astraddle a motor-bike? That would be unbearable. An older woman was one thing, but that young piece would be very hard to take. Or wouldn't be, which was the trouble.

No, this woman was no dolly bird. And even at this distance their relationship didn't look very affectionate, though they were standing close together. Caroline began edging her way round the edge of the games arena. The crowd was most tightly packed here and progress was slow, but at least she could keep Hazlitt in sight.

But now something else was happening. Two men had joined the woman and Hazlitt was quite enveloped in this little triangle. Caroline had been delighted to feel that the previous relationship had not been affectionate. Now suddenly she got an impression of menace which was multiplied as the little group began to move off away from the main Gathering. Then another figure detached itself from the crowd and began to move after them. It was the tall, bearded, Peugeot-driving Scot.

Convinced now there was something very wrong, Caroline tried to increase her speed of progress, but the crowd seemed set on hindering her. Exasperated, she ducked beneath the rope barrier which marked the edge of the track, ignored protesting cries from a couple of elderly stewards and began to sprint across the central arena.

It would not be a good idea, some still rational section of her mind told her, to get in the way of that man with the caber. But he, bulging muscles shiny with sweat and eyes tight-closed with effort and concentration, seemed determined that the encounter should take place.

A great shout went up from the crowd as Caroline dodged like a quarter back (or whoever it was that did the dodging in that tedious game) through the wondering competitors and officials and bore down upon the lumbering caber-tosser. The noise, and that instinct which says all is not right, finally caused him to open his eyes. Running directly towards him with menace written broad on her face was a girl. There was no way in which he could know the menace was not aimed at him. He turned at right angles, seeking escape, realised he was still carrying the caber, a considerable impediment to most normal methods of self-protection, and flung it forward as the easiest method of getting rid of it.

Fortunately there was nothing human to hinder its progress. What did lie in its way, however, was a table on which in bright and shining array stood the trophies. Cups for running; cups for jumping; cups for piping;

cups for dancing; and, of course, a large elegant, silver cup for caber-tossing.

The great length of wood smashed down on one end of this table, flattening some trophies and catapulting the rest high into the air in the direction of the crowd. Among them was a box, of no great intrinsic value, but containing the money prizes to be won that afternoon, ranging from 50p for the boys under-fifteen long jump (confined) to several pounds for the throwing events. After ducking out of the way of the heavier pieces of flying metal, the crowd seemed disposed to regard the descent of pound notes and coin as an acceptable compensation for the danger they had undergone and a version of the Eton Wall Game rapidly developed as they burrowed and scrabbled in pursuit of the spoils.

Caroline, meanwhile, had made the other side of the ground and broken through the ring of spectators there. Distantly she could see Hazlitt and his companions almost arrived at the car park. She tried to shout, but had little breath to spare. The squeak she managed, however, caught the attention of the bearded man, who was much closer than the others. He swung round and looked at her in some surprise. Over his shoulder she could see the others stepping over the rope barrier into the park and, working on the bird-in-the-hand principle, she flung herself desperately at the bearded man.

'What are you doing with him?' she screamed. 'You bring him back, you hear me? Bring him back!'

Easily he disengaged himself.

'A word to the wise,' he said. 'Keep out of this, lady. It's no' your speed.'

So saying, he turned swiftly away and mingled with the crowd. For a moment Caroline contemplated further pursuit, then looking behind her saw the welcome black-and-white check of a policeman's cap. It was time to get the professionals in, she decided, and began to trot towards it as swiftly as her laboured breathing would permit.

The policeman, it seemed, was just as eager to meet her. He ignored her attempt at explanation, her demands for urgent action.

'Name,' he kept on saying.

'Caroline Nevis!' she exploded finally. 'What's it matter if I'm Mary Queen of Scots? Are you going to do something?'

'Aye, I thought so,' said the policeman with grim self-commendation. 'Will ye come wi' me, please, Miss Nevis?'

Caroline would not have believed anything could have put Hazlitt's fate out of the top placings in her matters of immediate concern, not for a couple of days, at least. But ten minutes later, as she sat in the dark little police station looking at the copy of that morning's *Scotsman* which had been placed before her, her mind had only space for one thought: *How can this be happening to me?*

'Miss Caroline Nevis,' said the newspaper report, beneath a not very flattering picture of herself, 'failed to answer a shop-lifting charge at Lincoln magistrates' court yesterday morning. A warrant was issued, police went round to the house of her uncle, Professor James Nevis, well known for his television lectures on molecular biology. With his permission, they searched her room. A quantity of marijuana is believed to have been found. The police are eager to interview Miss Nevis who may at present be holidaying in Scotland.'

That was it. But it was more than enough. There was only one thing to be said.

'I want a lawyer,' said Caroline.

Suppose, thought Hazlitt, one were to marinade a piece of pork tenderloin in a mixture of malt whisky and heather honey for, say, two or three days, then bake it with a nutmeg in a case of choux pastry, what might that taste like?

He had always found the invention of new dishes a useful and profitable means of distracting his mind from external unpleasantnesses. Some of his greatest triumphs had been created in the dentist's chair.

But at this moment the digestive juices were refusing to trickle and the thought was beginning to predominate that unless something happened quickly, very soon he was going to be heading for that Great Kitchen in the Sky.

It had been foolish to appear so soon so publicly so close to his last place of disappearance. But that morning he had chanced on an old farmer having trouble with his even older car and by some miracle he had managed to poke the right wire to get it going. In gratitude the old man had shared the best part of a gill of whisky with him and offered to give him a lift to the Gathering. Like so many other disastrous decisions in his life, it had seemed like a good idea at the time.

Even when Tom (Mark II)'s woman had approached him on the field, he had been comparatively unworried. Surrounded by people, he felt safe. Why hadn't he thought of this before? All this business of bumming around on bog, mountain and moor was pointless. Crowds were the thing, especially when open assassination was not part of the plan.

So if Cherry had produced a gun, he had been ready to laugh at her and walk away.

Instead her two new friends had suddenly appeared, aubergine-ear had gripped his left wrist most painfully, while the other had produced a wicked little knife and described with graphic economy what he proposed to do with it.

Crowds, realised Hazlitt, were no use at all. All crowds could do was provide a ring of bewildered, nauseated, or frightened faces to stare down at some odd stranger lying on the crushed grass with blood and guts seeping from his belly. They might not even notice.

As he was hurried towards the car park he heard a great roar of excitement behind him. Doubtless someone had thrown a hammer or putted a shot or tossed a caber some extraordinary distance, while over here an ordinary man was getting into an ordinary car and being driven along an ordinary road to what was after all a very ordinary fate.

'And all this,' said Hazlitt, 'because of the Young Conservatives.'

'What?'

'You see,' continued Hazlitt, 'my mother made me join the Young Conservatives. And the majority of National Service officers were Young Conservatives. So by the time I got to Berlin in the fifties, I had had a bellyful of Young Conservatives. Oh yes.'

'Can't you shut him up?' asked Cherry. 'The sooner this is all over the better. I've left my sister looking after things and that means chaos.'

'If you and Sangster had been a bit more alert on Skye we'd have all been home by now,' said the knife man reprovingly.

'There's nothing like a bit of good old British inefficiency,' said Hazlitt. 'But let me get this straight. Sangster was the young man in the tartan shirt who threw me in the loch. Then the US cavalry in the form of, let me think, yes, the big chap with the beard turns up, is obliged to shoot Sangster, ties you up and pulls me out. How's that? I wake up and off I go. You somehow get back in the game and let your playmates here know what's going on. They set out to intercept.'

He looked around triumphantly, bringing a sharp pressure in the ribs from the automatic which had been substituted as a deterrent for the knife.

'Do we have to listen to this all the way?' demanded Cherry.

'Let the poor sod talk,' said the knife man pityingly.

If anything, Hazlitt preferred the woman's acrimony. At least it seemed based on a simple domestic longing to get home.

'I'm sure it's struck you,' he said, trying to prevent his normally rather high-pitched voice from soaring to the upper registers of fear, 'that whatever else intervention from our bearded friend shows, it shows that somebody knows what you're up to.'

'So?'

'So what's the point of doing it . . . getting rid of me . . . quietly when somebody else will know what's happened?'

'That depends who he is, doesn't it?' said aubergine-ear.

'You see,' explained the knife man, 'when you're found after your accident there'll be plenty of people who will *know* what's happened. There always are. But what will be accepted, of course, is what the evidence points to. It always is.'

'What about the police?'

'They're not involved.'

'Not involved,' snorted Hazlitt. 'When your buddy, Sangster, is found full of bullets, they'll be involved!'

'You underestimate Cherry,' said the knife man. 'They won't find Sangster, not for many a long year.'

Hazlitt looked at the woman, who ignored his glance —so much for domesticity. A long silence followed and he began to pay attention to the road. They were travelling east, he realised, following the contours of the coast. What their destination was, he didn't know, nor did he care to enquire. There are some things it is better to remain ignorant of.

'I could change my mind,' he said suddenly.

'What about?'

'About doing what they want. Suppose I agreed? That would make a difference, wouldn't it?'

'No,' said the knife man sadly.

'I mean it.'

'No doubt. I'm happy for you. Now I reckon the Roman Catholics are one of our biggest obstacles in the modern world, but I've got to admit the Inquisition had the right idea about eleventh-hour converts. They were delighted about it, praised God, gave thanks, but they still went through with the executions. Only now they were sending souls to heaven not to hell, which was nice. Alas, our own system doesn't hold out any such pleasant prospect for you. But it'll be a comfort for those who remain to know you returned to the fold before the end.'

'But I could be useful! That's what this is all about!'

'Look,' said the knife man. 'I don't know what this is all about, not precisely anyway. And I don't want to know. But I can tell you this—it's not what you will or won't *do* that's the trouble. It's what you know. Anybody can *do* things. That's why I like my job—I'm a *doer*. It's knowing things that's bloody dangerous.'

'I know *nothing*,' said Hazlit unconvincingly, and, staring out of the window, tried to concentrate his mind on the possible advantages of stuffing a tightly trussed quail with rosemary, basil, saffron, a head of garlic and a pound of wet uncooked rice, so that the whole thing exploded aromatically in the oven.

9

'Hello! Uncle James? Hello, hello!'

Suddenly Professor Nevis's voice came through loud and clear.

'Caroline, my dear. Are you all right?'

'Hello, Uncle James! Yes, fine. You don't know how great it is to hear you!'

So great, realised Caroline, that she had given him once again his childishly reassuring preface of 'Uncle'. But childish reassurance was what she felt like at the moment.

'What are you doing in that place—Durness, is it?'

'It's a long, long story. Look, what's going on down there, what's all this business about finding pot in my room? I don't use the stuff, I mean, you know that. They must have planted it. I don't know who. The police I suppose.'

The sergeant and constable who had moved discreetly to the far side of the office from which she was telephoning looked at her with hurt expressions and she blushed.

'Not, not you. I don't mean you. It's different down there . . . Hello, Uncle James? Sorry, I was talking to the policemen up here. They've been so nice, really, yeah. Great.'

Somewhat mollified, the policemen returned to staring out of the window.

'Listen, Uncle James. I'm worried about Bill. Bill Hazlitt, that's right. Yes, I've seen him. Up here, just before they arrested me. I think he's in some kind of trouble. No, I don't know what. No, I didn't speak to him either.'

'I think,' said Professor Nevis, 'that you must concern yourself with your own problems first, my dear. What Hazlitt is up to, no one knows. I know Stewart Stuart is most perturbed by his behaviour. Apparently there are all kinds of loose ends he left for his office to tie up as best they could. I fear he's done his chances of replacing Stuart little good.'

'It's not his career prospects I'm concerned about,' said Caroline with slight acidity. 'It's his physical well-being now, this minute. The police here have said they'll look into it, but I don't know what they can do.'

Hurt looks again from the window.

'I'm sure they'll do their best. But what about you, what arrangements have been made? Shall I come up, do you think?'

'No, don't do that. They're planning to send me back. That's right, isn't it?'

Nods from the window.

'Yeah. I think they were going to manacle me behind a train at first, but evidently they're sending someone for me, to see me safely home. Look, will you see about my legal rights, fix up a lawyer, that kind of thing? Tommy Poulson might be useful. Tell him I've been framed. And would you get in touch with the embassy for me? Start some big wheels moving, but ask 'em to play it cool, will you? I don't want any clever American correspondents sending a little piece about me back home to frighten Mom and Dad. *No!* Please, Uncle James. You mustn't ring them, not before you talk with me. It'll only upset them and I'm sure it's all going to blow over.'

'All right, my dear. I'm sure you're right. Everything will blow over. I'll find out at this end when you're getting back and see you as soon as I can. Now take care. And remember, *say nothing.* Goodbye.'

Poor old James, thought Caroline, replacing the receiver. He's really worried. What am I saying? *I'm* really worried!

'What happens now, Sergeant Shiel?' she asked.

'Well, Constable Craig here is going to drive you over to Thurso where ye'll spend the night.'

'Thurso! Why can't I stay here?'

'It's only a wee place we've got here, as ye can see, miss. And the night after the Gathering's often a very busy night for us. They can look after you better in a decent-sized toon.'

'I see. You want to keep us desperate criminals away from your common drunks, is that it? What about my car?'

'If you leave us your key, we'll see it's taken care of till ye can make arrangements for it to be collected.'

Craig went out and Shiel brought her a cup of coffee which she had to drink despite its heat and muddiness as it was obviously a concession to her nationality. She would have preferred whisky in a cardboard cup.

'I'm sorry to keep you from the Gathering,' she said.

'Never worry a jot,' he said reassuringly. 'I've seen too many to miss one. Aye, it's all for the tourist now, ye ken. And the laddie who goes around winning a' the big prizes for the hammer and the caber, why he's an Englishman!'

'You don't say!' answered Caroline. 'Look, Sergeant, okay, as far as you're concerned, I'm a criminal, under arrest. I say I've been framed. Twice no less! You might say I've been double-glazed! Now I know there's nothing you can do about it. It's something I'll have to sort out myself back in Lincoln. But this other business about

Mr Hazlitt, that's true, I promise you. It's not just a line I'm shooting to get me off the hook, if you'll pardon my metaphors. It's for real, and I can't afford to wait till I'm back in Lincoln to start sorting it out.'

She was trembling with earnestness as she finished her plea, and managed to spill her coffee. At least my words haven't been entirely in vain, she thought, as the ancient floorboards sucked up the khaki liquid like mother's milk.

'I've put out a call,' said the sergeant. 'Though you were far from detailed in your description of the people involved, 'cepting Mr Hazlitt, of course. But even if their car is spotted, which I doubt, as you're no' even sure about the colour, there's nothing we can do unless Mr Hazlitt indicates he would like assistance.'

'No. I suppose not,' said Caroline. 'It's a shit of a world, isn't it?'

'It sometimes appears so,' agreed the sergeant, unperturbed by her language. 'That sounds like young Craig now.'

A few minutes later Caroline was ushered into a tiny police van. There was no one around to see her departure. The Games were still in full Highland fling and even though the headland was out of sight, a vague rumour of applause and enjoyment was audible. The day was still very hot, but a smokiness had entered the blue of the sky and far away to the north like a mirage of Alps in a desert, vague ridges and peaks of cloud were beginning to emerge from the horizon's mistiness.

'We're in for a storm,' opined Sergeant Shiel. 'Watch how you go.'

Whether the instruction was aimed at Craig or herself, Caroline couldn't say. But she smiled sweetly at the sergeant, glad to have found at least one representative of authority whom she felt able to trust.

Constable Craig started the engine and the van began

to move swiftly along the empty road. Shiel watched for a moment, then went back into the station, shaking his head. Such a nice wee lass.

'You're quite sure she's safely out of the way, Durban?'

'Absolutely, sir. A very smooth operation, you'll be pleased to hear.'

'Smooth! She got within fifty yards of Hazlitt, you realise that? Which means within fifty yards of those three thugs. Thank whatever unhappy gods you worship that we've got her out of this safely.'

'Yes, sir. She was very determined, sir. And I would have had her arrested in Ullapool, only I was up so late slashing her tyres, I overslept this morning and . . .'

'Spare me, Durban, I beg you. Listen. Now you've finally got the girl off your hands, you'd better join up with Smithson and Campbell and give them a hand.'

'Yes, sir. Where will I find them?'

'How should I know? I am down here, don't you recall, while you are up there where it's all happening. They will be casting around for Hazlitt and the Three Stooges, I hope. Just find them and render whatever assistance you can. I hope they survive.'

'I'd be grateful for your help in this,' said Professor Nevis.

'Very willing to oblige,' said Tommy Poulson. 'And what about Hazlitt now?'

'He must look out for himself. Caroline's my concern at the moment.'

'Of course. Excuse me just a moment.'

He picked up his phone and dialled.

'Hello? Stuart? It was Sholto Greig, I wanted. Poulson here.'

'Greig's not here at the moment,' answered Stuart. 'No, he's not here.'

'Could you give him a message? We had a meeting

arranged this evening. I shan't be able to attend. I have
to go away unexpectedly.'

'Yes. I have that, I have that. Nothing unpleasant, I
hope?'

'I don't think so. Just give my apologies, will you?'

'I will. Certainly I will. Goodbye.'

Poulson replaced the receiver and smiled at Nevis.

'There,' he said. 'Now I'm all ready to go.'

Nevis did not return his smile, but sat with the glum
look of one who looks into a future that holds nothing but
unpleasantness.

'Haven't you got any imagination?' demanded Hazlitt.
'Surely you're not going to drown me again?'

'What do you suggest?' asked the knife man.

'Couldn't you maroon me on a Pacific Island with a
tribe of over-sexed Amazons and let nature take its
course.'

'Let's get it over with,' snapped the woman.

The four of them were seated in the car, like a typical
English family group on a day's outing whose high point
is eating soggy sandwiches in a seaside car park. The sea
was certainly here, about ten feet forward and sixty
down. But there the resemblance to an English seaside
scene ended. For a start the sun was still hot, the sky
bright blue. And theirs was the only car in sight on this
grassy headland.

'There's going to be a storm,' said aubergine-ear, looking straight ahead to the threatening horizon. Hazlitt
explored the remark for concealed threats. Ever since
they had turned off the main road and bumped and
bounced their way to this present situation, he had been
alert to every nuance of every comment. There could
only be one reason for stopping and it wasn't so that
the passengers could relieve themselves.

In the end he had brought up the matter himself by

his comment to knife man (whom the others referred to as Sandy while aubergine-ear was Chuff—whether derived from the bird, the engine sound or the naval idiom was not clear). It slowly became apparent that the discussion of the best method of disposing of him was more than just a bit of ghoulish humour. It was a real problem. They wanted an accident, but without their personal involvement as witnesses. As a lonely camper on the shores of Loch Coruisk he had been an ideal subject. But now having made a public appearance at the Games —and also possibly having been seen leaving the Games in his present company—a more subtle solution was called for.

'He's a very good swimmer,' commented Cherry dispassionately. 'You'd need the bandages again.'

'Then you've got to pull him out and take them off. It's a bit risky here, isn't it?'

'I suppose so.'

'Lots of bird-watchers about on a day like this,' said Hazlitt. 'See for miles. Probably a pair of binoculars on us at this minute.'

'Shut up,' said Sandy equably. He opened the door and got out. The momentary draught was refreshing. Chuff got out also, saying to the woman, 'Watch him.' She nodded and fractionally increased the pressure of the muzzle of her automatic against Hazlitt's rib-cage.

'You wouldn't really shoot, would you?' he said testingly. 'I mean, you don't want a corpse with lead in it and a car covered with blood.'

'Shut up,' said the woman. 'All I want is to get done and get back to my kids before my bloody sister ruins 'em.'

The continuous revelation that Cherry had a normal humdrum everyday existence bothered Hazlitt.

'You've got a family?' he said, unable to keep all the incredulity out of his voice.

'What do you think I do, spend my life running around dark alleys with a gun?'

'No. Of course not. I'm sorry. I never thought . . .'

The two men had strolled to the edge of the headland and were peering down, deep in conversation. Now they returned to the car.

'No,' said Sandy. 'It's not high enough. And the water's only a few feet. No rocks.'

'Oh hell! Couldn't we knock his head?' said Cherry.

'It wouldn't work.'

'What a bloody waste of time!' she snarled.

'Look, come and see for yourself. Chuff'll watch Laughing Boy.'

Cherry opened her door and slid out as Chuff stood politely by, waiting to take her place. Hazlitt watched, his mind a turmoil of fear. All right, so this place and this time might not suit. So they would go elsewhere. And every minute and every mile took him nearer death.

Cherry stooped forward in the door prior to standing up. Her backside was offered to him, a tempting target. He reacted like an underprivileged Italian, seized a healthy handful of flesh and squeezed it hard.

The woman shrieked and staggered forward, lost her footing, stumbled and grasped at Chuff. To attempt to leave the car and run for it was obviously pointless. To sit there and have his face slapped by an indignant Cherry was equally pointless. The only action to take was the one that his subconscious survival mechanisms had decided on seconds earlier, but which his conscious mind refused to contemplate. He gave it no chance.

He leaned forward and released the handbrake. Instantly the car began to move forward down the gentle grassy slope. Chuff and Cherry disentangled themselves and looked after it, the former with gentle bewilderment, the latter with righteous indignation. Only Sandy was stirred to action and ran alongside the slowly moving vehicle trying to reach in through the open window and put the brake on once more.

Hazlitt clenched his right hand with the knuckle of the middle finger protruding from the fist (an attacking style much favoured in his dimly remembered schooldays) and drove this sharply into Sandy's wrist.

'Hell!' exclaimed the man, withdrawing his arm quickly. He continued to trot alongside the car, peering in at Hazlitt and shouting. Gradually there dawned in his face the suspicion that this was no accident but an attempt at escape. Hazlitt, watching the edge of the cliff approach at a terrifying speed (15 mph, perhaps, but it felt terrifying), could understand the man's problem. As an escape attempt, it was little short of suicide.

With a stoicism bred of numbness out of terror, he placed his spectacles in his shirt pocket, lay down on the floor behind the front seats, and awaited the event.

It all looked quite dramatic to the watchers on the shore. The car ran elegantly over the edge of the headland, seemed to pause there for a moment like a diver balancing himself before he plunges from the board, then the bonnet dipped forward, the boot flipped up, and it was gone.

Hazlitt had surprisingly little sense of a change of direction. His eyes were tightly shut and he had wedged himself firmly beneath the seats. There was a slight sinking feeling in his stomach, a kind of splodgy crashing noise, an increase of pressure against the front seats. But the first real indication that waiting-time was over and doing-time had arrived was the shock of icy water flooding in through the windows and engulfing his body in a trice.

It was bone-crackingly cold, despite the heat of the sun. It took more than a couple of fine days to influence these seas. Fortunately, water was an element in which he had always felt perfectly at home and now he reached for the car door without panic and pressed the handle.

Nothing happened.

He pressed again. Still nothing. Now he began to feel panic. Oh Christ! Suppose the blasted thing had been buckled by the impact? His lungs were beginning to ache. He tried again without success. He could hold out for only a few seconds more. What was best? Try another door, obviously. But turning round in a car full of water was not the easiest of tasks .Various bits of luggage had slid forward from the rear sill and were hindering his leg movements. He felt it should be some consolation that drowning in this car should make it impossible for Sandy, Chuff and Cherry not to be connected with his death. But it wasn't. Indeed he felt a sudden urge of affection for the trio, a desire to see them all again.

He managed to turn, reached the other door, the one through which he had helped Cherry. It must be open, indeed hadn't been closed after Cherry's exit. It *was* open! He pushed. It moved six inches and stopped. It felt like a solid, unarguable stop and a short-sighted glance through the sunshine-filled water told him why. That side of the car was up against a large shell-ornamented boulder.

I'm going to die, he decided. Without ever having been to Acapulco; without ever having tasted *paté de canard en croûte*; without even having told Caroline how much I love and desire her. I'm going to die and there's nothing I can do to prevent it.

Except lift the door handle *upwards* instead of pressing it *downwards*.

He turned again, lifted the handle and the door opened slowly through the resisting water.

A few seconds later he broke the surface, sucked in huge delicious lungfuls of North British air and looked up at the three heads protruding over the edge of the cliff like a display of traitors impaled on London

Bridge. Whether the expression on their faces was one of relief or disappointment, his myopic gaze could not make out.

It made no difference. Here was where he did not want to be.

He trod water and undid his laces, kicked his boots off, turned on to his stomach and began to swim due north.

Thirty minutes later he tried to turn for the shore, but found himself in the grip of a current so strong it was pointless wasting his strength by wrestling against it.

He began to feel faintly worried. He knew he could keep afloat for hours, but it was a rather pointless exercise unless he were actually going somewhere.

And when the waters gradually started to swell mightily under him, and the blue of the sky was washed over with fast-moving whites and greys, and thunder began to roll from one end of the constricting horizon to the other, he began to suspect that with unintended kindness he had saved his enemies the trouble of arranging their little accident for him.

10

To her surprise Caroline had no difficulty in going to sleep in the small, comfortless cell the Thurso police provided for her. Her new guardians were polite but cold in their attitude and she felt with the disappearance of Constable Craig that she had lost a friend.

She lay down on her bed, thought briefly of the horror with which her mother would view her present plight, wondered what it was that Hazlitt had done to invoke the intervention of forces powerful enough to frame her like this, said a small but fervent prayer for his safe keeping, and fell asleep.

Not even the terrible storm which had exploded over the sea in the early evening and which raged all night disturbed her rest.

Next morning attitudes seemed to have thawed a bit. She had a feeling that someone somewhere had dropped a hint that she was not, after all, a wild, anarchist, drug-pushing drop-out, but a hitherto law-abiding and respectable citizen for whom the American embassy would be deeply and genuinely concerned. Surprisingly, the thought did not so much comfort her as make her feel old and bourgeois.

They let her sleep until well on into the morning, which surprised her.

The escort from England had not yet arrived, her

WPC told her, with some sighing and shaking of heads at another example of southern inefficiency. Meanwhile would she care for kippers for breakfast and a look at the desk sergeant's newspaper?

Yes, she said to both questions. The kippers were excellent, the paper (a local journal—the national dailies, like her English escort, were still on their way) rather dull. Egotistically she searched through it for any reference to her own arrest, but found none. But as she was putting the paper aside to concentrate on her kippers one item tugged the corner of her eye.

A car had plunged into the sea on the coastline between Durness and Thurso. Left unattended, its handbrake must have slipped and the driver and passengers had watched helplessly as the white shooting-brake slid quietly over the cliff.

Into Caroline's mind's eye slipped a vivid picture of Hazlitt being hustled towards the car park by two men and a woman. A detail not remembered before was now quite clear. In the car park directly in their path was a large white shooting-brake. So distracted had she been thereafter, first by the bearded man and next by Constable Craig, that she had not seen where Hazlitt was taken. But now, like an old painting under the hands of a renovator, her memory was coming up bright and clear. The white shooting-brake had gone, she was sure of it, by the time Craig had escorted her from the Games arena.

Or had this item in the paper in fact created the memory rather than merely restored it?

The cell door opened and her policewoman came in. Her friendliness seemed to increase as Caroline's departure drew nearer.

'He's arrived,' she said. 'But never worry, finish your breakfast. The poor mannie looks worn out and he's taking a cup o' coffee himself.'

'Thanks,' said Caroline. 'Say, I was just reading about this car that rolled into the sea. You have to deal with things like that?'

'Oh that. Aye. Damn' fools. Lucky they were no' in it.'

'They?'

'Aye, two men and a woman. They were trespassing anyway. The farmer whose land it was spotted them standing by the cliff's edge. When he found out what had happened he rang us. They didna seem best pleased.'

'There were just the three of them? No one else. In the car, I mean.'

The WPC laughed.

'Och no. They'd have been worried about that, even these three. No, the car was sticking well out of the water at low tide and we got their luggage out. It's gey damp, naturally, but it'll dry. I'll leave you to finish your breakfast now. Five minutes do you? Good.'

She went out. Caroline pushed aside her plate and stared unseeingly at the paper. If these were the people who had taken Hazlitt, if he had still been with them when they drove on to the headland, if the car had not gone into the water by accident, if . . . She pulled herself up short, realising that she was merely multiplying conditions in order to avoid conclusions. Or, rather, one particular conclusion.

She turned the pages of the paper noisily as though she could shake away her fears. Here on the back page were the *Deaths* and *In Memoriam* columns. Not much help there. She looked away from them. Stop Press. News from Stromness, Orkney. A party of fishermen had returned late the previous evening, having been caught in the storm. With them they had brought an unusual catch. A man, completely exhausted and on the point of collapse. He had almost been tossed on board by a huge wave. They had wrapped him in blankets and fed him with whisky. It was then he uttered the only words he had spoken since his rescue. 'Highland Park, 100 proof?' he had asked. The unidentified man was at present under medical care in Stromness. No report had yet been received of anyone lost overboard during the storm.

A flood tide of joy rose in Caroline's heart. As certain as she had been about the car in the sea, just so certain was she now that this unidentified half-drowned man was Hazlitt.

The joy overflowed in tears just as the cell door opened. Two voices spoke.

'Good morning, Miss Nevis.' Cool, professional.

'Caroline, are you all right?' Concerned, indignant.

She looked up through tear-misted eyes.

Standing in the doorway was Inspector Servis, the man who had talked to her in Enoch Arden's back in Lincoln a hundred years ago.

Beside him and much more welcome was Tommy Poulson, as grey and vague-looking as ever, but with real concern written in his face.

'Hi, Tommy,' she said with attempted casualness, and was distressed to find her tears of joy becoming real tears in the end.

Poulson explained that he had been contacted by Professor Nevis with a request first for advice and then for active assistance. Nevis's own solicitor was of a background which hardly equipped him to deal with young American girls on drug charges, and of an age which made the prospect of such a journey unthinkable.

'James seemed to feel that even though I don't actively practise law, my acquaintance with you made me a suitable adviser. I had nothing else on at the moment, so here I am. I hope you don't mind.' Poulson sounded genuinely worried lest his presence should be offensive.

'Tommy, it's just great to see you. Great,' Caroline assured him, meaning every word.

'Thank you. There's nothing I can do here, of course, except travel back with you. The inspector has been most kind and agreed to this.'

Servis nodded, his face expressionless.

'Can I talk with you alone, Tommy?' asked Caroline.

It was Servis who answered.

'It's a difficult position, Miss Nevis. Mr Poulson is here as a friend rather than your legal representative. Or so I read the situation. He's not a practising solicitor, are you, sir? I thought not. I think in the circumstances that I must exercise my right to be present at any interview you have.'

'Can he do this, Tommy?' demanded Caroline.

'It's debatable, at least,' said Poulson. 'But I think here and now's not the place to debate. Let's get you back home where we can fix up bail and then you can talk with anyone you want.'

Caroline looked uncertainly at the two men. Her fears for Hazlitt were such that she felt an urge to confide in either of them, Poulson as a friend or Servis as a professional. But somehow the thought of explaining to both of them at the same time that a couple of paragraphs in a local paper had convinced her that Hazlitt, narrowly escaped from death, was lying in a Stromness sick-bed, was beyond her.

'If you're ready, miss, we've a train to catch,' said Servis politely.

'I'm ready,' she said, standing up. 'You know, Inspector, one thing bothers me. Do you *know* I've been framed, or are you just some kind of useful mug?'

She did not stay for an answer but marched rapidly out of the cell and along the corridor which led to the main area of the station. As she passed through the next door, the WPC stepped forward to greet her.

'Chin up, eh?' she advised. 'Here's your bag with your things. Just check them, then sign for them at the desk, will you?'

A quick glance in her bag assured Caroline that her assortment of credit cards and panties had all been returned and she leaned on the desk to sign her receipt.

Beside her, a middle-aged man with ginger hair was talking to the desk sergeant.

'It's a write-off,' he was saying. 'The garage went out this morning and the storm had smashed it to pieces.'

'Aye well, sir. It's a sad way to end your holiday. But it's lucky you were all out of the machine.'

Caroline's ears pricked. Casually she glanced towards the man. Surely this couldn't be one of Hazlitt's kidnappers?

'Here's your friends now,' said the sergeant.

From the back of the station appeared a man and a woman carrying some sea-stained suitcases. This was more like it! thought Caroline. The woman looked angry enough for murder and as for the man with his swollen left ear, he looked evil enough for anything.

'It was kind of you to dry them out for us,' said the ginger-haired man.

'All part of the service, sir,' smiled the sergeant.

As though in answer to his name, Inspector Servis now appeared beside her.

'All taken care of,' he said. 'Let's go. There's a car ready for us.'

Caroline's last sight of the three figures at the desk was not comforting. Ginger was still in conversation with the sergeant, the woman was glaring at him impatiently, while the man with the thick ear had picked up the sergeant's newspaper and was casually glancing at the back page.

Again she thought of talking to Poulson and Servis and paused on the steps of the police station to assess the possible consequences. If Hazlitt wanted the police to be involved, he could have done it himself, she thought. And perhaps in any case the trio wouldn't spot the Stop Press item.

'Let's go,' said Servis behind her.

Outside everything was damp and fresh after the storm. The morning sun had not yet had time to do its repair work and the concrete of the steps still gleamed wetly. She took a pace forward, her foot skidded and she tumbled untidily on to the pavement.

Poulson and Servis were there in a flash. 'Are you all right?' asked Servis.

'Are you hurt?' asked Poulson.

She tried to stand up.

'Ouch! Oh hell! I've done something to my ankle.'

Servis looked down at her anxiously.

'I'll fetch a doctor,' said Poulson.

'No, it's okay,' said Caroline gamely. 'I'll manage. Where's the car?'

'It's round the side,' said Servis. Caroline thought it might be. There was a little cul-de-sac alongside the station where Constable Craig had parked the previous evening. She rose, leaned heavily on Poulson, and began to hobble along the pavement.

'Hang on,' said Servis. 'I'll go and fetch it.'

He set off, paused uncertainly at the corner, and disappeared from sight.

He was only gone for half a minute but when he returned the situation had altered radically.

Poulson, looking very surprised, was lying on his back on the pavement. And Caroline, her sprained ankle miraculously healed, was sprinting away down the street like an Olympic two-hundred-metre finalist. This impression of great athleticism was rather spoiled as she rounded a corner with a Chaplinesque series of hops, but her speed must have picked up again immediately, for when Servis reached the corner, she had disappeared completely.

Breathing hard, he leaned heavily against the solid grey stones of the Bank of Scotland building and implored God to sod all bloody Americans to eternal damnation.

Caroline, inside the bank, watched him obliquely through the mullioned window and wished she could lip-read. Then, because to do nothing in a bank is odd and she needed money anyway, she sorted through her supply of credit cards and approached the counter.

Twenty minutes later, after a nerve-racking zigzag trip down the main shopping street collecting goods and information, she left the town by bus. Scotland, her brief experience told her, was full of young girls wearing slacks, anoraks, floppy tartan berets with large pom-poms, and carrying all their earthly belongings in a duffel bag. She had joined their ranks. And the bus she was on was heading for Scrabster where, her informants assured her, she would find the Orkney ferry.

They were right. Queues of cars were edging their way forward to be hoisted precariously on a sling and dropped into the guts of two ships. Caroline joined a group of young people and walked unchallenged past a policeman who was examining all pedestrians with grim thoroughness. Only one of the ships carried passengers and it was the other which left first, causing a little unease among some of the drivers whose cars were on it. But finally the growing medley of noises around Caroline rose to a climax of departure and Scotland began to drift away from her. She let it go without a qualm and looked to the north and the open sea. It smelled of freedom. She could have shouted with joy, but the gulls tracking the ship's wake seemed to be shouting it for her.

Two hours later, as the Old Man of Hoy rose tumescently to starboard, she began to feel qualms, the gulls' cries became derisive and her breakfast kippers seemed eager to rejoin their native element. She recalled that her mother made some modest claim to *Mayflower* descent, but her present feelings convinced her that no one in her family could have survived weeks on the Atlantic in a small wooden boat.

The ship dipped slightly and her stomach rose violently. There were people on both sides of her and she turned away in search of a more private bit of rail. A few feet away she saw a sight which put her own ailments out of her mind for a moment. Leaning against the rail were the two men and the woman she had seen that morning in Thurso police station.

It was small comfort that they looked as ill as she felt. She had hoped that they would not spot the news item at all, or at least would not have caught today's ferry. But here they were, heading as quickly as she was for Hazlitt lying helpless in a hospital bed.

She stumbled away towards the bows of the ship, worry and seasickness fighting a war of attrition inside her. She wondered whether she might be better off inside and hesitated at a door which led into the ship's bar. It opened as she stood there and she had to jerk back to avoid being struck.

'Sorry, lassie,' said the man who stepped out. She recognised him instantly. It was the man with the beard from Skye.

Her pom-pom hat postponed his recognition for a second only.

'Well hello!' he said. 'It's you again! Man, but you look ill!'

'I'm fine, thank you,' said Caroline with sturdy American independence, finding it difficult to keep her feet.

'I know what you need,' he said with a grin that showed strong white teeth through the blackness of his beard. 'The Scottish panacea. John Barleycorn.'

'What?'

123

> ' 'Twill make a man forget his woes;
> 'Twill heighten all his joy;
> 'Twill make the widow's heart to sing,
> Tho' the tear were in her eye.'

He seized her arm as he declaimed and pulled her through the door. For a moment she thought the change of atmosphere and the crush of people would make her sick instantly. But her mind, eager for familiarity, quickly began to arrange these new surroundings into the familiar context of any saloon bar in any pub on any Saturday night. As long as she didn't look through the windows and ignored the shiftings of the floor, she could cope with this and she was beginning to feel better already before the bearded man thrust a glass of amber liquid into her hand.

'This'll make your heart sing,' he said.

'Thanks, but I'm no widow,' she answered. She drank it; it was good.

'No, you're not,' he said, looking at her with worry in his eyes. 'Tell me, why are you going to Orkney, Miss Nevis?'

'Just a holiday visit, Mr ... er ... ?'

'Campbell. Lackie Campbell.' He paused, seemed to make up his mind about something and spoke once more. 'I think we're after the same thing, Miss Nevis. And we both think we'll find it on Orkney.'

'And what's that, Mr Campbell?'

'Hazlitt.'

'Oh. And what's your reason for looking for him?' asked Caroline, surprised at her own self-control.

'The same as yours, I suspect.'

'My God!'

He shook his head, grinning.

'No, I don't mean I love him. But I want to protect him. He's got nothing to fear from me, but there's others

124

who'd be glad to see him put under the ground. Believe me, Miss Nevis.'

'Who are you, Mr Campbell?' she asked

He drew her into a corner and pressed up close against her so that she could feel the heat of his body through her anorak and slacks.

'I can tell you because I doubt if you'll believe me,' he murmured. 'I work for British Intelligence Counter-Espionage. Aye, there you are, I can see it in your face.'

'What you see in my face is a wish not to be ravished in such a public place. That may be a masonic grip you've got on my left thigh but it's telling me nothing.' She sighed with relief as he backed off a little. 'That's better. Okay, so you're a secret agent. Prove it.'

He shrugged.

'Sorry,' he said. 'They don't give us certificates. Suppose I buy you another malt. Will you believe me then?'

'It'd help.'

Surprisingly, it did. She found herself quite taking to Lackie and after only a little bit of prompting she described her adventures since last they had met at the Durness Gathering.

'Aye, I'm sorry about a' that,' he said as she described her arrest and incarceration.

'What do you mean, you're sorry?' she said suspiciously. 'Hey, you don't mean you've fixed all this?'

'Oh no. Not me personally, you understand,' he protested. 'But it sounds like the kind of thing the department would do, just to keep you out of harm's way.'

'I'll sue the bastards! All this mother-of-democracy guff. I'll take it to the United Nations!' She was genuinely indignant. Campbell just grinned at her.

'Anyway,' she continued, 'what's Bill supposed to have done?'

'Bill?'

'Hazlitt.'

125

He looked around at their nearest neighbours, who were a young couple impelled by fatigue, sickness or lust into each other's arms, and a thickset man with his nose buried in a Guide to the Orkneys. Then, dropping his voice, he said, 'He's a spy.'

'A *what*?'

'Shh! It's okay. He's one of ours. Not very important, not till recently anyway. Then he stumbled on something big.'

'Big?'

'Aye. Well, big enough to stand on someone's toes.'

The mixture of metaphors suited Bill, thought Caroline sadly. Stumbling around standing on someone's toes.

'And these people are trying to kill him?'

'For God's sake, lassie, can you no' keep your voice down to less than a rebel yell? Aye, that's the strength of it. I managed to save him on Skye. But we got parted and like yourself I've been on his track ever since. Once I can get to him, I can protect him. Will you help me?'

'Well, sure,' said Caroline. 'But how? I mean you know as much as me. Or more perhaps? I'm just guessing this man in the hospital is Bill. You may know it for certain. Do you?'

She looked at him eagerly, hoping to have her guess confirmed, but he shook his head slowly.

'No, I canna say for sure. But it seems likely.'

'Yes,' she said, disappointed. 'Yes. I hope it is. And I hope we reach him first.'

'First?'

'Before the others. For God's sake, don't you know they're on board as well?'

Clearly he didn't. And clearly he was far from happy to make the discovery.

'But what's the problem?' wondered Caroline. 'Couldn't you have them arrested or something?'

'No, no. We don't work like that, you see. Nothing which would bring us to public notice.'

He finished his drink and looked through the window.

'Not to worry, eh? We're nearly there. It's just a matter of moving quick, that's all. Don't look so glum. It'll be fine, you'll see. *Come what will, I've sworn it still, I'll ne'er be melancholy, O!*'

'I'd be careful or you'll make your bosses suspicious,' said Caroline. 'I believe Burns is very popular in Russia.'

'So he is,' Campbell said with a laugh. 'Let's form a queue at the gang-plank. Or, rather, you form a queue. I'll keep out of sight—they know me, you see. But never fear, I'll be close behind.'

A queue had already formed, though it was another fifteen minutes before the ship docked at Stromness. By a dint of much pushing and elbowing, Caroline contrived to be first down the gangway and set off along the quay at a good lick. There had been no sign of the seasick threesome and she hoped that their malaise would occupy them for some time to come.

The other ship, she noticed, had also arrived and most of its cargo of cars were parked along the quayside. A pity in a way. It had been an amusing thought that the ship might in fact have headed down the coast to Aberdeen where the cars were all sold at a criminals' auction.

At the end of the quay stood a policeman. Caroline paused. Just how efficient had they been in Thurso? Pretty efficient, she answered herself, especially with an angry Servis roaming around the place. Which meant that there was a strong possibility that some of the shop-keepers had told of selling an anorak, a duffel bag and a tartan beret to a young American; perhaps her en-quiries about the Orkney ferry had been passed on too; perhaps the bus conductor recalled having to change a pound note for her fare.

The policeman was advancing. British policemen advanced differently from American policemen. American policemen looked conscious of their Western lawman heritage. They advanced alertly, suspiciously, ready to go for their guns if trouble broke out. British policemen had much more of majestic inevitability about them. If they hit water, they would keep on walking, through it or on it.

He's coming for me! Caroline was suddenly convinced. She glanced back. The quay was now full of people. Enough to sweep her by unnoticed? she wondered. It was not a risk she dared take, not now she was so near Hazlitt.

She stepped sideways into the row of parked cars awaiting their owners. Their keys were all in. They had to be, of course, otherwise the car ship could not be unloaded till all the passengers arrived. Perhaps all the good people of Stromness had a mad half-hour of hell driving before the ferry came in? It must be a great temptation.

It was, and she succumbed. Nearby was a flashy two-tone Cortina GT, complete with ostentatious GB plates, motoring club and county badges, cellophane bullet-holes, comic window-stickers, dangling dolls and a nodding-headed plastic Alsatian. Some people deserved nothing but the worst. She climbed in, started the engine and like the first away at Le Mans, blasted out of the line of cars, rounded the policeman on a brake-screaming arc and roared off along the quay.

She found herself momentarily nonplussed when she reached what she took to be the street. It was paved with large flagstones and looked much more like a pedestrian pavement than a thoroughfare for vehicles. In other circumstances it looked a fascinating place to explore, wandering off most invitingly in either direction. But Caroline had no idea which way to go. She wound down the window and shouted at a group of men sitting in silent communion with each other on a bench outside a shipping office.

Courteously one of them rose and made his way to the car. Oh hell, thought Caroline. What do I ask for?

'Excuse me,' she said. 'I'm looking for a hospital. Or a clinic perhaps.'

The man looked concerned.

'Is it the seasickness?' he queried in a pleasant accent which was at the same time sing-song and guttural.

'No, not for me. Someone I know . . . a man was picked up by a boat last night, now where would they take him?'

'Ah yes. The drowned man.'

'Drowned? You mean he's dead?' Her heart contracted to a walnut of pain.

'No, no. Just drowned, not dead,' said the man. 'They took him there.'

He pointed. Caroline followed his finger, still fearing to see a funeral parlour at the end of it. Instead she found herself staring at a splendid three-storeyed building, like an Edwardian villa gone mad, which bore the title on tarnished gilt letters: 'Hamnavoe Hotel'.

She nodded to herself. Yes, that would be it. Even half drowned, Hazlitt would have himself taken to the best hotel.

'Thanks,' she said, getting out of the car. It might as well stay here where its owners could easily find it. She slammed the door and the Alsatian nodded inanely at her.

The bottom storey of the Hamnavoe was devoted exclusively to bars, she discovered. It seemed a sensible arrangement. On the next floor she found a reception desk. A pleasant open-faced man greeted her, enquiring after her accommodation needs.

'No, I don't want a room,' said Caroline. 'A guy was brought here last night, I believe. Picked up at sea.'

'Ah,' said the man, who seemed to be the manager, 'Mr Coleridge, you mean.'

Oh God, thought Caroline. Coleridge!

'Yes, that's him.'

'He should really have gone to hospital, you know. But he was most insistent that he should be taken to a good hotel. A doctor was called, of course, but apart from fatigue he seems to have been all right. Extraordinary bit of luck, though, being picked up like that. Sailing to the Shetlands in a small boat's just not on, even at this time of year. You're a friend, are you?'

'I'm his daughter,' said Caroline.

Coleridge indeed! Sailing to the Shetlands! He was not the only good liar in Stromness.

'I'll take you along to his room. This way.'

He set off up the stairs to the next floor, Caroline following. This place had really been built for a statelier age. The corridors and stair-wells were all wide enough to take a sizable motor-car with ease. Perhaps that's what the locals did with all those tempting cars off the ferry!

'Here we are.' The manager halted outside a nice solid-looking door and rapped hard on it.

'Mr Coleridge. You have a visitor.'

There was no reply and the manager turned the handle. Slowly the door swung open and suddenly Caroline was terrified that perhaps she would be faced by a real nautical Mr Coleridge, unfortunately shipwrecked while sailing to the Shetlands.

Instead a more disturbing sight met her eyes. The room was empty. The bed had been recently slept in, that was clear, but of Hazlitt or Coleridge there was no sign.

'How odd,' said the manager. 'Perhaps the bathroom ...'

But Caroline was not interested in the bathroom. Her

eyes were fixed on the pair of spectacles which lay on the thick carpeted floor. She bent and picked them up. They were his, all right. Those lenses were unmistakable. He would never leave voluntarily without these.

They got here before me! she thought in panic. Somehow the threesome got here before me and they've taken him.

'Are you all right?' asked the manager anxiously.

'Yeah. Sure. I'm fine,' she said.

It had to be the police now, she decided. And quick.

A strange noise came from somewhere. She glanced at the manager, but it plainly was not him. It had been a kind of surprised, puzzled grunt.

She looked round the room. Slowly, like a perfectly made prop for a horror film, the door of the huge mahogany wardrobe swung open.

Standing inside, eyes screwed up in short-sighted puzzlement, clad in a huge pair of pyjamas and clutching a bottle of Highland Park 100 proof malt whisky menacingly in his right hand, was a bearded figure she hardly recognised for a moment.

'Ah, there you are, Mr Coleridge,' said the manager brightly. 'Here's your daughter come to visit you.'

Meeting after such adventures and in such circumstances they should have fallen into each other's arms and then into the very convenient bed.

Instead Hazlitt stepped out of the wardrobe, took his spectacles from her hand, put them on, peered into her face, said, 'My God! Caroline!' and poured himself a large shot of whisky.

The manager, unperturbed at this strange reunion, smiled approvingly and left.

'What the hell are you doing here?' demanded Hazlitt crossly. 'I thought it was . . . well, never mind.'

Absurdly Caroline found herself starting to stammer out an apologetic explanation. She pulled herself up short, took a deep breath, and exploded.

'Listen, fatso!' she said. 'I've been charged with shop-lifting and drug-taking! I've been arrested and jailed! I've been chased, harried and seasick! I've assaulted Tommy Poulson and I've stolen a car! All to get to you before those other three. But as far as I'm concerned now, they can have you and welcome!'

She hoped to appeal to his conscience, but instead touched a more sensitive area.

'Those three? Which three? What do you mean?'

'The three who took you away from Durness. Two men and a woman.'

This produced an agitation in Hazlitt she had not

seen since Tarquin or Sholto had asked him if he was commissioned during the last war.

Making faint mewing noises, he ran around the room in little spurts and dashes like Harry Langdon in the old movies, finally coming to rest at the wardrobe.

'You're not getting back in there?' queried Caroline in some alarm.

'Clothes! They've taken my clothes!' protested Hazlitt.

'Well, they must have been pretty damp,' Caroline pointed out.

'What have you got in there?' he demanded, eyeing her duffel bag greedily.

'Nothing really,' she said opening it. 'Would a pair of panties be any help?'

'Slacks!' he said. 'Take your slacks off.'

'What!'

'Take them off!' he commanded, dropping his pyjama pants and dancing impatiently before her.

Is this how it happens then? wondered Caroline, slowly unzipping her slacks. What became of the moonlight and violins?

'Come on!' he said, pushing her back on the bed and dragging the garment over her ankles.

'Bill,' she said anxiously, 'you will marry me, won't you?'

'What? Are you mad or something? Give me a hand!'

Hazlitt was having difficulty getting into the slacks which were designed to fit a slimmer leg than his, but with a great effort he succeeded. He tucked the pyjama top into the waistband and pulled up the zip as far as it would go. Fortunately it was at the side, which meant that modesty was not very much endangered.

'What about me?' asked Caroline, standing up and looking at her bare legs forking provocatively from under her anorak.

'Mini-skirt,' said Hazlitt. 'You wear them all the time. You haven't got a spare pair of shoes, have you?'

'No!'

He immersed his tiny feet in a huge pair of carpet slippers, sighing deeply at her lack of preparedness.

'These will have to do. Money?'

'Yes.'

'Give me five.'

He laid the note on the pillow, picked up his bottle of Scotch and headed for the door.

'Come on,' he said.

'Where?'

He looked at her disparagingly.

'Anywhere,' he said. 'Remember. If *you* can find me, anyone can find me. Let's go.'

It was not an assessment of her achievement that she much cared for, but something about Hazlitt's stealthy air communicated itself to her and she postponed her protests.

The huge corridor was empty, but voices were audible coming up the stairwell.

Dominant was the manager's.

'Mr Coleridge is looking much better. His daughter's visit has probably cheered him up a lot as well. He'll be delighted to see you all, I've no doubt . . . quite a family party . . .'

What particular relationship the threesome had claimed with him, Hazlitt did not care to find out. Seizing Caroline's hand, he dragged her along the corridor and through a door which led to a smaller flight of stairs, which took them down into the kitchen where a chef was basting a saddle of beef.

Hazlitt sniffed.

'Enough's enough,' he said to the man. 'You've overdone it. This way I think.'

They left the kitchen, and joined the main stairway.

'It's the Scottish disease,' said Hazlitt. 'They overcook everything. Here we are!'

They burst out of the hotel doors and stood on the steps looking down at the paved street. Caroline recognised in Hazlitt her own indecisiveness of a few minutes ago. Across the road at the entrance to the harbour the Cortina stood where she had left it. Its rightful owners seemed to have appeared and were in angry conversation with the policeman whom Caroline had so feared on arrival. The owners, a middle-aged man and woman, were making themselves plainly heard even at this distance.

'We haven't come all this way on those bloody awful roads just so some peasant can take a joy-ride in our car!' protested the man in a vaguely Londonish accent, while his wife kept up a burden of long drawn out *That's right* and *Yeses*.

As they watched, the policeman, probably exasperated by the noise these two were making and the attention they were attracting, ushered them into the shipping office in search of privacy.

'Come on,' said Caroline.

'Where?'

She did not answer but dragged him over the road to the Cortina. The little group of people round it made no attempt to hinder them as she opened the door and climbed in, though Hazlitt's strange garb caused a stir of interest.

As the engine burst into life, three things happened. The door of the shipping office opened and the car owner reappeared, his face red with incredulous indignation. And out of the hotel rushed Chuff, Cherry and Sandy, while behind the car from the pier appeared Lackie Campbell.

Caroline thrust her foot down on the accelerator, spun the wheel hard right and unceremoniously crashed her way into the line of traffic making its way from the ferries.

'I think,' she said as they left behind the narrow streets of Stromness which had been restricting her to a mere 70 mph, 'I think you'd better start telling me what this is all about.'

Hazlitt eyed her assessingly, wondering what lie he could tell her.

He's wondering what lie he can tell me, thought Caroline.

'Take the next left,' said Hazlitt. His acquaintance with Orkney was a very vague one, based on a single visit at least twelve years earlier. And when he set out on his swim from the sunken car he had had no intention of renewing it. When the storm finally broke he had been convinced that the end had arrived and not even thoughts of halibut, rubbed with lemon juice and thyme and dried and smoked over a cherry-wood fire, were able to still the fear fluttering in his belly. Then he heard voices, and the fishing boat had appeared and the next wave had practically spilled him aboard.

'Where are we going?' asked Caroline. 'And why not just tell me the truth?'

The two questions were not in any way connected and sadly Hazlitt recognised the foolishness of trying to pretend they were.

'I'm not sure,' he admitted to both questions. 'If we'd kept on going we'd have ended up in Kirkwall, the capital, which is where we don't want to be with a stolen car. I assume you *have* stolen this car?'

'Yes,' said Caroline. '*We* have stolen this car. Are you complaining?'

'No. I suppose not.'

'Then stop sounding so bloody condescending. It's your blasted fault if I've plunged into criminality.'

'Stepped,' said Hazlitt. 'For most Englishmen it's a

137

plunge. For most Americans it's a mere step.'

'Well, you certainly seem to have plunged pretty deep.'

'Not at all,' said Hazlitt. 'It's in order to avoid plunging that I've come to this pass.'

'You're still not *telling* me anything!' protested Caroline.

'Let us first dispose of this car,' said Hazlitt. 'Then we'll find a ditch to sit in and exchange confidences.'

They drove on in silence, Caroline leaving the job of car disposal to Hazlitt. Finally he tapped her on the arm with one of his irritatingly authoritative gestures.

'Over there,' he said. 'There' turned out to be a rather primitive car park just off the road. There were half a dozen cars in it already and Hazlitt made her manœuvre the Cortina until it was as well hidden from the roadway as possible.

'Good place to hide a car is a car park,' he said.

'Clever,' said Caroline. 'You sound pretty expert.'

'You soon develop an instinct,' said Hazlitt, rummaging around in the back of the car. 'Ah! we're in luck. Yesterday's picnic!'

He produced a carrier bag containing some apples, a meat pie, a packet of biscuits and a bottle of lemonade. Probing even more deeply beneath the traveller's debris, he emerged with a pair of low-heeled women's shoes which fitted him nicely and an orange windcheater which was far too big.

Caroline felt herself alarmed. So far all they had done was use a little petrol. Even people with dangling dolls and nodding Alsatians had rights.

'You're not going to steal that stuff?' she said.

'No,' said Hazlitt. 'Purchase. Money, please.'

'You're being very free with my cash,' she said, but handed over her purse.

'Let me see,' said Hazlitt. 'Apples, say tenpence. Biscuits the same. One cellophane-wrapped pie—they should pay *us* to eat such things—but say fivepence. And for the lemonade. Shoes, two pound? Say two-fifty. Windcheater three-fifty. That makes a grand total of six-thirty, call it seven. There we are. Better leave the key in the ignition. Hope no one steals it. Or finds it, for that matter. We may need it again later.'

He clambered out of the car, resplendent in his new gear.

'Fit? Then let's go.'

'Go where?' demanded Caroline, wondering for the first time why people should want to park their cars in such an unlikely spot. There was little evidence of human habitation nearby.

Hazlitt pointed to a sign with an arrow pointing in the direction of the sea. It read SKARA BRAE.

'What is Skara Brae?' asked Caroline, following Hazlitt along a springy turf path.

'A neolithic village,' explained Hazlitt. 'Just the place for an American scholar and an English administrator to have a tête-à-tête.'

They arrived at the shore, pausing by an old building on the edge of the grass-matted sand-dunes. An attempt had been made to shore it up against the ravages of the tide, but it looked as if it were probably too late. About a furlong away they could see a mound which seemed to house the remains of the prehistoric village. Some people were standing on top of it peering down into the ground. A man in a shiny peaked cap was talking and pointing.

'Let's sit here for a while,' suggested Hazlitt. 'You can have a look at the remains later.'

Despite everything he's not going to miss a chance to drag me round some more antiquities! thought Caroline wonderingly. Her friendship with Hazlitt seemed to have developed in, among, or upon a series of ruined abbeys, tumbledown castles and shabby stately homes.

'You first,' said Hazlitt, making himself comfortable on a large grey stone and taking a bite out of an apple.

Caroline told her story swiftly and with little interruption.

'You *hit* Tommy Poulson?' said Hazlitt at one point.

'Well, yes, I don't suppose he'd have tried to stop me running away, but I didn't want to make any trouble for him. So I made it look good by hitting him, you follow?'

Apart from this, Hazlitt let her reach the end of her narrative without comment and Caroline was a little piqued at the lack of 'Oohs!' and 'Ahs!' of amazement at her courage and ingenuity. Listening to her own story as she talked, it sounded pretty good.

'Your turn,' she said now. 'And, remember, the truth!'

'I told the trio it was the Young Conservatives,' said Hazlitt slowly, 'but it all really began, I suppose, in the Army.'

'The Army?' said Caroline. 'My God. You mean Sholto and Tarquin were right? You did fight in the war?'

Quickly she tried to work out how old this meant Hazlitt must really be.

'No!' he said long-sufferingly. 'National Service. I did two years in the early fifties. I was in the RAF. They taught me all about radar and I spent most of my time in West Berlin, before the Wall, of course. It was a curious thing, National Service. For most people the only way to survive the boredom, the debasement and the homesickness was through some excess or other. Drunkenness was the popular favourite. And a lot of people got religion, for instance. Me, I got communism. We had an enthusiast on the station. He introduced me to some locals. Nice people, they made me feel at home. It gave me somewhere to go at weekends, real houses with home comforts, that sort of thing. After a year I was quite happy to tell them anything they asked about my work.

Christ, it was so completely unimportant! I was a radar technician, what did I know? I'd had to sign the Official Secrets Act, but that didn't mean much more to me than having my religion officially registered as C of E.'

'What?' said Caroline.

'Church of England,' said Hazlitt. 'You were either that or Roman Catholic. Well, nothing happened really. I spent two years rather more pleasantly than I would have done otherwise, then returned home and went up to university. Oxford.'

'You mean there are others?' mocked Caroline.

'Try not to be frivolous. I was still a communist, you understand. It seemed a rather clever thing to be and there were lots of other rather clever young men who all clearly felt the same. But Oxford offered opportunities for other things than working for the cause. And privately I was losing a bit of enthusiasm when I was invited to meet someone rather important in the party. The Man. That's how I thought of him. He had no name. He was a big man, almost bald, with piercing grey eyes. Very impressive. We sat and talked for a long time. I was on my best dialectic behaviour, of course. He seemed particularly impressed by my willingness to pass on the non-secret secrets of my military experience.

'Well, nothing happened for a few weeks, then I was sent for again. This time it was suggested to me that in the present climate of witch-hunting which surrounded party membership—the backwash of McCarthyism was still being felt at that time—it might be useful if some younger members who seemed likely to achieve high success in their careers should seem publicly to have left the party.'

'My God!' said Caroline. 'You mean they wanted you to become a "sleeper"?'

'I see you have the terminology off pat,' said Hazlitt.

'I was a little more naive in those days. Yes, really. I mean, I didn't think in terms of spies or subversive activity, that kind of thing. I was flattered by the implication that one day I would be in a position of influence, and it seemed sensible to conceal anything which might affect my chances. So I left the party. It was fairly easy to do. A gradual break, confirmed when Hungary happened a couple of years later and people were dropping out like apples in autumn. I set about being a young lad about Oxford, having a good time. I did it very well. So bloody well, in fact, that at the end of the three years I was quite obviously far too frivolous for the Diplomatic Service and failed miserably by both exam and interview. Then I got a real taste of what I had let myself in for. I met the Man again. He was furious. I was far too nervous of him to tell him that I reckoned that spiritually I had really left the party. But I managed to declare that I couldn't see myself in the Foreign Office, still less in politics, and that I was considering trying university administration.

'Well, we parted amicably and I began my long and distinguished career. It's absurd, but I never imagined *they* could really see me as a potential Burgess or Maclean. It didn't begin to dawn on me until 'sixty-three and Philby. Then suddenly for the first time I realised how narrowly I'd missed the same kind of demands being made on me! And I complimented myself on having entered a sphere of work totally uninteresting from the Man's point of view. I know it would have been better to make a clean break even then, but that required more nerve than I possessed. All that seemed necessary was to lead the life of an apolitical gourmet, so I thought *whatthehell*! I mean, I *was* an apolitical gourmet! The trouble was, I got interested in my work and started to do well. And the real trouble started after I did that stint in Balowa eighteen months ago. I did a good job and got on well with the people I met from all walks of life. Among them was Colonel Oto, whom I'd met a couple of times in Oxford in the fifties when he too had seemed to be an apolitical gourmet. He didn't seem all that much different as an army colonel, not till they had their little bit of bother last December and he emerged as top man.'

'Are you going to eat all those apples or can I have one?' asked Caroline.

'I'm so sorry,' said Hazlitt, passing the bag.

'Spare me the phoney apologies and make the story,' said Caroline.

'Well, they wanted me back at Balowa University this year, as you know. Everything had quietened down and I was happy to go. In fact I felt quite pleased at being specially invited by the president. Then I got the call.'

'The call?'

'Yes. I had to go and see the Man again. I'd no idea what it was about, but I went. Why not?'

'You must have been mad!'

'Perhaps. We talked. I prevaricated a bit. Not all that much. It's remarkable how easy it is to have good communist principles in the comfort of an English University! The crunch came, as I thought, after a couple of hours. Would I be willing to do the party a small service in Balowa. What? I asked. Just pass a message. No danger, no complications. A once only thing.'

'And you refused,' said Caroline.

'Oh no. I agreed! Why not. It seemed a little enough thing to keep them happy. And I couldn't really believe that these little espionage routines either helped or hindered anyone.'

'You say you *used* to be naive!' said Caroline. 'If you'd have been a girl, you'd have got laid first time out!'

'I know nothing of such things,' said Hazlitt primly.

'All I wanted was a quiet life. No trouble. I was thinking of settling down. Or was that naive too?'

'Depends what you had in mind,' said Caroline casually, the apple sticking in her throat. He ignored her invitation and went on.

'No, the real trouble started when I found out what they really wanted me to do.'

'Not just pass a message? I thought not. What then?'

'Assassinate Oto.'

'Jesus!' said Caroline, swallowing half the apple at one go. 'You're putting me on!'

'Afraid not. Of course, I demurred. They thought I was just concerned for my safety, assured me that there would be very little danger. They didn't want me to shoot Oto or blow him up, nothing like that. No. All they wanted me to do was poison him. They had some stuff extracted from a cassava fruit, whatever that is. Kills with all the symptoms of alcoholic poisoning—Oto's a pretty hard drinker. It's incredible, isn't it?'

'You've said it! My God, Bill, what did you do?'

'What would you have done?'

'I don't know. Let's see. I'd have got in touch with CIA or something. What's the English equivalent?'

'MI something. Well, I didn't need to. I told the Man I'd need time to think, and British Intelligence got in touch with me. I had to laugh, really. They knew everything about me, right from my days in Berlin! Some "sleeper"! My cradle had been carefully watched over by just about everyone in the game, it seemed.'

'And that was when they recruited you,' said Caroline, nodding as the pieces began to fall into place.

'When they what?' He sounded surprised.

'You don't have to act coy,' said Caroline. 'Campbell told me on the boat, remember? Or didn't I mention that bit?'

'Told you what?'

'That you were working for British Intelligence. Look, why don't I just head back to Stromness, pick up Campbell and bring him back here? With him around, you'd be safe enough, surely.'

Hazlitt began to laugh. While it was pleasant to see him regain a little of his old jollity, Caroline was not altogether happy about the laugh.

'You mean Campbell doesn't work for British Intelligence?' she asked, puzzled.

'Oh yes. He certainly does that.'

'And didn't they want to recruit you?'

'They certainly did. And still do, I believe.'

'Well then.'

'I don't want to be recruited. I don't fancy it one little bit. Not for me; no, it's not for me.'

'For Godsake!' snapped Caroline. 'You left it a bit late to jump on your moral high horse, didn't you? Okay, so you don't want to go around assassinating people for the Reds. But helping one of your own government's agencies doesn't exactly make you a fascist reactionary pig, does it?'

'Perhaps not,' said Hazlitt. 'The only thing is, *they* wanted me to kill Oto as well.'

12

The people visiting the ruins had finished now and were moving back towards the road.

'Fancy a look?' said Hazlitt, rising and pulling Caroline to her feet.

They walked along the stony beach hand in hand. Overhead the sky was blue, and the shore and the sea were bathed in a light of such clarity that it seemed to enter into and inform all that it touched.

'Poor old Oto!' said Caroline. 'Doesn't anyone like him?'

'Only me,' said Hazlitt. 'And quite a lot of Africans. But they don't count, of course. Once again I demurred. It was pointed out to me firmly but politely that if they wanted, they could see me put away for a couple of years.'

'Framing seems to be their speciality!'

'Well, I did break the Official Secrets Act twenty years ago,' said Hazlitt. 'They pressed me hard, wanted information—I had very little—and names.'

He paused. Caroline glanced at his normally cherubic face and thought how haggard he was looking.

'You had names?'

'A couple. Contacts had to he made. I'd kept my eyes open, put two and two together.'

He fell silent again.

'So you gave the names?'

'Well, no. No, I didn't feel able to. They'd done me no harm. I could see no reason why ...'

The light on the sea and land seemed to enter Caroline's mind.

'It's someone you know! Someone at the university?'

He released her hand.

'Listen, Caroline, I can't talk about it. In fact, I've talked too much. I don't want you to get involved.'

'You're a bit late, aren't you?' she mocked.

'Perhaps. But at least no one's trying to get rid of you permanently! I told both lots that I wasn't playing ball, you see. And got an ultimatum from both. That was bad enough, but worse was that the party found out that the intelligence lot were on to me.'

'Why was that worse?'

Hazlitt laughed.

'If British Intelligence don't trust me, they just put me in jail. But if the party want rid of me, they've got to be more final! No one was sure which way I would jump. I wanted a breathing space, so I dug out my old camping gear, topped up with stuff from Enoch Arden's and set out for Skye. Untraceable, I thought! And that's the story of my life.'

'Oh, Bill, what are we going to do?'

He was touched by the *we* and took her hand again. But there was no hint of a long-term solution in his mind. The immediate problem loomed too large. Safety for Caroline—and for himself, survival.

'We are going to look at Skara Brae,' said Hazlitt.

To her surprise, Caroline found herself enjoying the next half-hour. She was sure they ought to be doing something else and at first paid little attention to the custodian's description of the village, which consisted of the remains of seven huts connected by narrow alleyways.

No roofs remained and as the huts were buried to the tops of their walls in what turned out to be a stone-age midden heap, it was possible to walk around well above living level and peer down.

In several of the huts there was an erection of stones —three uprights topped by a slab on which the same arrangement was repeated—which she took to have some unfathomable religious significance, rather like Stonehenge. It wasn't until their guide referred to it as a 'dresser' that she realised that the four recesses formed by the structure were in fact cupboards. In here some neolithic housewife had kept her cooking utensils alongside her husband's more warlike instruments. This simple domestic fact brought the place alive for her and after the custodian had finished his patter and retired, she and Hazlitt stood peering down through the glass roof which had been put over the most perfectly preserved of the huts.

'An uncomplicated kind of life,' she said, almost enviously.

'Up to a point. They had their troubles too. Remember, they were driven out of here by a sandstorm and they never came back. We at least can go back.'

'I hope so,' said Caroline.

They left the site and strolled along the beach till the horn of the bay hid them from any subsequent visitors.

'We're being very casual,' said Caroline suddenly. 'What's the plan?'

Hazlitt took off his glasses and mopped his forehead with the nine inches of pyjama sleeve which persisted in slipping down over his hands. Far from being casual, his mind had been working furiously for the past hour to arrive at the best course of action.

'Here's what I think,' he said in his best Vice-Chancellor's committee voice. 'We've got to get back to the mainland somehow. That means either the ferry from

Stromness or a plane from Kirkwall. I know nothing about the air services, but the ferry leaves about nine o'clock in the morning. Obviously it'll be watched . . .'

'You mean the police?' interrupted Caroline.

'For you, the police. I'm not a wanted criminal, am I? But there'll be others looking for me. Now, I don't expect they'll be on the alert till the ferry starts being loaded. If we get to the pier in the early hours of the morning it shouldn't be difficult to slip aboard and hide until the other passengers start arriving.'

Caroline was dubious.

'How do we get back to Stromness?' she asked.

'We hang around here till it's dark,' said Hazlitt. 'Then I check whether the Cortina's been spotted and removed. If not, we drive gently to the outskirts of Stromness and abandon it once more.'

'And if it has been found?'

'Then we walk. It's only seven or eight miles. A couple of hours on a fine night.'

'I thought you might say that,' said Caroline bitterly. 'Why the hell couldn't you have gone into hiding somewhere nice like San Francisco. Nobody walks in San Francisco.'

'Which is why most Americans are pasty-faced asthmatics,' said Hazlitt triumphantly. 'Apart from the walking, what do you think of my plan?'

'It stinks,' said Caroline. 'It's a rotten plan.'

Secretly Hazlitt agreed. It was an absurd plan. What he really intended to do was rather more complicated and not very nice. He was going to steal all Caroline's money, abandon her and let the police know where they could pick her up. Despite the altruism of his motives, he did not view the prospect with any great pleasure. One of Caroline's blind spots was her refusal to recognise his infallibility. When the time came—if it ever did come —to explain himself, he anticipated trouble.

150

'What do we do in the meantime?' asked Caroline. 'Till it gets dark?'

Hazlitt looked around. They were in a little fold of land running down to the ocean. A grassy bank with a slight overhang made it a natural place of concealment. The sun was in decline but still very warm. He reached into the carrier bag and produced his bottle of Highland Park.

'Let's sit down,' he said. 'I'm sure we'll think of something.'

'Any news of Caroline?' enquired Nevis anxiously.

'Nothing,' said Poulson.

'Oh God. And Hazlitt?'

'Nothing there either. But everyone up here's working on it.'

'I know, I know. Do your best, please, Tommy. Promise.'

'Of course. But if she gets in the way when we catch up with Hazlitt she'll just have to take her chances,' said the young man.

'At least give instructions she's not to be harmed, if possible,' said the grey man.

'I'll do that. But I won't jeopardise the whole exercise just for her sake. You understand that?'

'I understand,' said Stewart Stuart. 'You won't reconsider? Everything's run so smoothly here until these last few weeks.'

'No. Hazlitt's in my way,' said Sholto Grieg. 'I was worried long before the African business came up. You knew that. I've no desire to do his work for him.'

'Ambition's a killer,' said Stuart sadly.

'Yes,' said Sholto Greig.

The Reader in Moral Philosophy plunged deep into the dark waters of the pool, slid torpedo-like along the bottom till he saw the outline of a body above, and broke the surface beside it.

'Tarquin,' he said, 'we can't go on meeting like this.'

'All right!' said the Old Etonian angrily. 'I've had quite enough. Quite enough. I don't suppose Durban's showed up yet? I thought not. Well, you and Smithson will have to manage yourselves. Just bring him back, that's all. I'm tired of subtlety. If you tread on his toes a bit and he shouts out any names, I won't object. The girl? Her, too, I suppose. But no fuss. Please, no fuss.'

He slammed down the receiver and looked around the room, wondering as he had often done in the past whether his masters had got it bugged. It seemed likely. They were not men given to easy trust.

Anger rose again, turning back the years like the elixir of life, till he was a Yorkshire schoolboy again.

He blew a long and loud raspberry and went out in search of a drink.

It was nearly midnight before Hazlitt decided to move. Caroline was asleep with her head on his chest. To leave her to wake up in this lonely spot and discover he was gone would be too cruel, he decided. But he seized the opportunity to steal her money. Caroline, he reasoned, would be safely in the hands of the police who would feed, shelter and transport her back to Lincoln where, after a bit of token finger-wagging, the charges against her would probably be quietly dropped.

He meanwhile would also be making his own way south by a less public route. There was a man he wanted to see. Running had been stupid. Reason was now due for a turn. If he was important enough to chase and kill, for his silence, then he was important enough to keep alive for it. As for the threat of charges under the Official Secrets Act, that was surely risible. After twenty years what kind of case could they bring?

His sleeve extension flopped down as he tried to close Caroline's purse and she awoke. Gently he dropped the unclosed purse back into her duffel bag.

'Time to go,' he whispered.

She sat up and gave a huge yawn, which, as she stretched out her arms and realised how stiff she was, turned into a groan.

'My God,' she said. 'The Puritans were right. We certainly pay for our pleasures.'

'Quite right too,' said Hazlitt. 'Well, let's toddle off, shall we?'

A nearly full moon hung heavily in the sky. The broad plate of its light was cracked and fragmented by the sea and after a few moments they found they could see almost as well as in daylight. Though what they saw, thought Caroline, pressing close to Hazlitt, now seemed very different in form and presence. A wind had sprung up off the ocean and moved through the coarse sea grass like a living thing. Rags of grey cloud were fluttered across the face of the moon. And the custodian's building by the ruined village sat dark and squat as though by night it took the function of guardian on to itself.

For all that, it was a kind of comfort to reach it and feel that something man-made was close at hand on this strange non-human plane of shifting air and sea and sky. But Hazlitt's words were not comforting.

'Right,' he said in his best Officers' Selection Board (Failed) voice. 'You wait here while I check on the car.'

'Are you crazy?' hissed Caroline. 'If you think I'm staying here by myself . . .'

'Just for a minute,' assured Hazlitt. 'I can move much more quietly by myself and if there is a bobby sitting up there waiting, we don't want to disturb him, do we?'

Yes, please, thought Caroline, in whose mind flashed a sudden picture of her cell in Thurso with all the nostalgic potency of the slave's dream of home. Hazlitt thrust the almost empty bottle of whisky into her hands and kissed her lightly on the forehead.

'Pip-pip,' he said, and moved swiftly away.

'Bill!' said Caroline tremulously, but there was no reply.

'Oh, Bill,' she said to herself miserably, and sitting down on the custodian's doorstep tried without success to convince herself that it was impossible to detect a note of finality in a 'pip-pip' and a kiss on the forehead.

Hazlitt was tortured by guilt as he made for the road. His reason told him no harm could come to Caroline. When she became worried by his non-appearance she would head for the car park and look for him there. By which time if, as he expected, the Cortina were still there, he would be miles away and phoning the police. Once in their hands, she would be absolutely safe.

He made little attempt to conceal his presence till he saw the white scar of the road, then moved with greater caution towards the park. The car was still there, he saw with relief. Despite his enthusiasm for exercise, he had no real yearning to be afoot that night.

His experiences during the past few days had taught him to take nothing on trust and he did not approach the car directly, but moved round the park in a series of concentric circles, making absolutely certain that no reception committee lurked in the long grass. Satisfied, he crouched low and darted swiftly across the tyre-beaten turf towards the Cortina.

As he reached it and put his hand out to open the driver's door a sense of something not quite right struck him and he paused. All looked well. In the darkened interior he could see the key still in the ignition as they had left it. What then?

Imagination! he told himself and took hold of the door handle. Then in the corner of the eye on the rear sill he saw the model Alsatian nodding its head in idiot welcome.

Even as his mind pumped out all the possible implications, it was too late.

A figure rose from the floor at the back, in its hand a dully gleaming automatic.

'*A man may drink and no' be drunk, a man may fight and no' be slain*, but I wouldna bank on it,' said Lackie Campbell. 'Will you no' step inside for a wee chat, Mr Hazlitt?'

I'll count up to one hundred, thought Caroline, and that's it. I'll wait no longer.

She began counting, slowly at first, accelerating rapidly from about twenty to forty, then with deliberate self-control returning to her first measured counting for the last fifty.

That's it, she thought, and began to rise from the doorstep.

Somewhere close by she heard a noise.

The night was full of sounds. Wind in the grass, sea pulling at sand and stones, the cry of sea birds out on some unimaginable late mission.

But this was different. Why it was different, she could not tell. What the noise had been was itself not clear. A twig snapping? Hardly. There were precious few trees on Orkney. One stone struck against another? Perhaps.

But it didn't matter. What did matter was her certainty that it was a man-created sound.

Hazlitt returning. Her heart flooded with relief. What else could it be? But still she did not move out of the shelter of the doorway.

Then she heard a voice. Hazlitt's voice, she tried to reassure herself. But unless Hazlitt's admittedly high-pitched voice had risen several tones further, unless Hazlitt was walking along talking to himself, and unless Hazlitt had doubled round so that he was approaching the site from the same direction as before, this was not Hazlitt.

Worse, there was a hardening suspicion in her mind that she knew exactly who this was. Or these were. For now the sound of at least two people walking and talking could be heard. It was some comfort that they were making very little attempt at concealment.

She crouched down on her haunches, then bobbed forward, rabbit fashion. It was very uncomfortable. Hazlitt would have been pleased, she thought. Most of his recreational activities seemed to involve a certain degree of discomfort.

To make room for the custodian's building, a section had been cut out of the mound in which the remains of the huts were set and Caroline now crouched at the end of the natural wall so formed and carefully peered round the corner.

Her care was very necessary. Sharply she drew in her breath. She had been right. It was that popular music-hall threesome, Cherry, Chuff and Sandy, in person. And they were no more than five yards away.

'This is stupid!' proclaimed the woman, who was obviously in a very bad humour. 'I told you he wouldn't hang around near the car. He's long gone.'

'You're probably right,' said the man Caroline now knew as Chuff. Even in the moonlight his swollen ear could be spotted. 'But we had to look.'

'Well, we've been a mile that way and a mile this and I'm damned if I'm going any further!' said Cherry.

They must have walked by us while we were sleeping! thought Caroline, horrified.

'All right,' said Sandy. 'It's late and we've been wandering around for more than an hour. Let's head back to Stromness and get some sleep. We'll need to be up early in the morning to check the ferry.'

'What a farce,' said Cherry. 'He can't be that important, surely. He struck me as being a pretty futile little man.'

Caroline felt herself swelling with indignation at this gratuitous attack on Hazlitt. Fortunately Sandy put at least part of her thoughts into words, saying, 'He can't be all that futile, can he? He's given us the slip a couple of times and survived things that would have killed me. Let's not underestimate him. He's important enough to kill and slippery enough to escape. That's all we need to know.'

'What about this blasted girl?' grumbled Cherry.

'She's not to be hurt unless absolutely necessary,' said Sandy. 'Special orders.'

'That's what I mean. We can't even get on with the job properly! And it's my kids who are suffering.'

Up you too! thought Caroline, shocked at this lack of female solidarity.

'Come on. Let's go,' said Sandy. They began moving forward again. It was time to retreat. She did her rabbit trick again, bobbed back to the doorway and pushed herself as far into the shadows as possible.

Her leg struck something cold which moved. Her throat constricted with fear and she thrust out her hand in an instinctive sportsman's movement which Hazlitt would have been proud of.

Her fingers settled round the neck of the whisky bottle just before it tumbled off the doorstep. But not soon enough to prevent a small clinking noise.

She froze. It had, after all, been a very small noise. Surely no one would be interested in such a minute noise.

'Over there,' said Cherry. 'Didn't you hear?'

'Oh, stop being so damned nervous,' growled Sandy. 'And come on!'

A grunt of protest cut off short came from Cherry, then there was silence broken only by the sound of footsteps receding along the shore.

Thank God they're tired, thought Caroline. But it wasn't very professional of them, for all that. In their shoes, well it was hard to imagine herself in their shoes, but what *she* would have done was . . . shut Cherry up, then pretended to move off without suspicion, but in reality let only one of their number move away, trying to make enough for three, while the others . . . suddenly it became important not to stay in this little trap of a doorway any longer.

Grasping the whisky bottle firmly in her left hand, she slid out of the doorway and began to edge her way carefully down the side of the building. Her duffel bag was over her shoulder and while it was a bit of an encumbrance, it was a lot better than leaving it as firm evidence that somebody had been hiding there. Only when she turned the corner and put the whole building between herself and the sea did she remember the carrier bag.

They had finished all the food hours earlier—and Caroline had noted that despite his scorn of it, Hazlitt had devoured at least two-thirds of the meat pie. The bag had almost been left behind, but Hazlitt was a compulsive protector of the countryside and had remembered it after only a few steps. Normally Caroline would have been completely in accord with his anti-litter attitudes, but now she wished he kept the countryside as untidy as he kept his flat. (Anyone who married him, she thought parenthetically, would have a hell of a job house-training him.)

Of course, it might still pass for ordinary tourist debris. But one thing was certain—its discovery would prompt a wider search. She had to get away from the building and keep out of sight.

She pressed close against the wall and strained her ears. All the noises of night crowded in on them, harmonising with her own desperately controlled breathing and wildly pulsing blood till she could not distinguish the external from the internal. A sound that might have been a carefully muffled footfall came from the left side of the building. She could only trust her instinct now and instinct told her to move fast.

She headed right, scrambling up the steep side of the mound in which Skara Brae was set. How much noise she made she could not tell. At least she was out of that hole. But now instinct said that she had to find another one. Up here she was an eye-drawing lump against the skyline.

Slowly she began to push herself backwards, her eyes still fixed on the rear wall of the custodian's building. It was deep in shadows, a black contrast with the moon bright tiles on the roof. But she had no doubt at all when a new lighter shadow merged with the others. She thrust herself back with all her strength, the ground fell away beneath her body and she rolled down into one of the passages that ran between the huts.

Here she crouched for a moment, half of her mind longing for Hazlitt to return, the other, and still stronger, half praying fervently that he wouldn't.

Again it was time to be on the move. She still couldn't tell whether she had been detected or not. Either way, retreat was the best policy.

The passage was deep enough for her to walk upright without risk of detection from anyone not on the mound. But animal instinct was practically in full control now and she crouched low as she moved.

For the moment safety lay down here in these ancient remains. But something else was there too. The almost sudden awareness she had experienced in the afternoon that human beings had lived, loved, given birth, cooked, eaten and slept here now returned. Not quite the same now. Then in the light of day it had been an awareness of domesticity, a shock of recognition across the ages, an outgoing of affection. Now it was different. True, beings distantly related to herself had lived here, but they had died here also. Bodies had been found here buried beneath the walls so their ghosts would sustain them. The last educible use made of Skara Brae had been as a burial ground. And the last living inhabitants of the village had fled in panic and terror as the great Atlantic gales set the dunes in motion and forced the blinding abrasive sand down passages and through doors like embalming liquid into the veins of a mummy.

Now panic and terror could easily return to Skara Brae. Caroline recalled the custodian telling her that a trail of beads had been found along one of the passages and that the archaeologists theorised that one woman in her terror had broken her necklace as she squeezed through the narrow door and the beads had fallen unnoticed in her flight to safety. The odd thought came into Caroline's mind that perhaps somehow she was related to this woman. Not impossible. Hazlitt would be amused. Another example of American ancestor worship. Whatever the case, Caroline hoped that the neolithic girl had made it.

She paused once more with no real idea of where she was and glanced back. Nothing. And down here it was so silent. Silent as the grave. A handy thought.

She looked up now and though darkness was her friend, wished that more of that glorious silver moonlight could spill into this pit.

As if at her command some way behind her a light flickered momentarily into being, stabbed down into the passage and disappeared.

Someone was on top of the mound and using a torch. In one way this was a comfort. Such open searching could mean they had pretty well decided no one was there. But the chances of detection were much increased.

She hastened forward. Here the passage went underground for a short way and it took an act of will to leave the moon and stars behind. But again and again with increasing frequency the torch beam was flickering above.

Caroline stopped again. Unless her pursuers actually descended into the passageway, she could not be found. She could hear their footsteps now, beating dully on the turf and coming to a halt almost right above her.

'Satisfied?' demanded Sandy.

'Let's go,' answered Cherry, avoiding direct agreement. 'This place is creepy. I wish to God I was in front of my own fire. I bet that sister of mine's turned the house into a shambles.'

'Right. Hey, Chuff! There's nothing here. Let's be on our way.'

Chuff, Caroline surmised, had been the decoy sent ahead along the beach to give the impression they had all gone. She was glad it had been him. For some reason based purely on her couple of sightings of the threesome, she feared him most of all. Cherry seemed bad-tempered and understandably irritated by the whole business. Sandy seemed quite a reasonable sort of fellow. But Chuff . . . She shuddered and thanked heaven he had not joined the search.

The footsteps above were moving away now, leaving her alone with whatever uncomprehending ghosts inhabited the site. For a second she felt an absurd impulse to call them back, just to have human company.

And even more absurdly it was for their assistance that she screamed as Chuff's hand seized her by the hair and dragged her violently backwards.

It was a double bluff, she thought miserably, as she

twisted herself round, clawing the walls with her right hand in an effort to keep her balance. I saw through it once and thought I'd won for ever. I'm no use for this game.

But even as her mind admitted defeat, her body opted for survival like her pretended neolithic sister of three thousand years before. She swung her left hand at Chuff's head. It would have been an ineffectual hook had it not been for one thing. With a diligence that Hazlitt would have admired, she was still carrying the whisky bottle.

Oh my God! Bang goes his other ear! she thought in horror as Chuff released his hold and half fell to the floor. She made a small movement forward to administer first aid, realised that the object he was trying to drag from his pocket was a gun, heard the rapidly returning footsteps of the other two above, and fled.

Behind her the gun spoke. Television and the cinema had accustomed her to the sound of gunfire, both real and theatrical. Not until this moment, however, did the reality of the fear such a sound could cause occur to her. Newsreels might take her to Asia or Africa, fill her with revulsion, outrage, horror—or on occasion boredom—but the sound of Chuff's gun put every cell in her body at the red alert of terror.

She heard the bullet scrape along the wall beside her. Then she was round a corner and running wild.

Someone descended with a thud into the passageway behind her. That left one above. One too many. A voice, Sandy's she thought, shouted, 'No guns!' A comfort if it penetrated Chuff's two thick ears. She saw a narrow opening to the right and thrusting herself in, crouched with her whole body shaking like a peal of wedding bells. Her new pursuer approached, did not pause, was past in an instant. She could not see who it was, did not want to see, did not care if she never saw again any member of that monstrous race who could hurl hot lumps of lead at her soft and defenceless body.

But he had stopped. There was a long silence, more terrible than any that had gone before. This time it was real silence. Here in this stone-deadened tunnel no noise seemed to penetrate. Not the wind or the sea or the rustlings of life in grass and air. Only, now, the sound of footsteps returning.

She retreated into the tunnel, stooping low. It must lead into one of the open huts, but there was no attracting glimmer of light at the end of it. Then the ground was no longer under her feet and she fell forward into a pool of absolute blackness.

Instantly she rolled on her back and sat up, trying to force her sight through the darkness. The tunnel by which she had entered was completely lost to her. She had no way of understanding where she was and she heard a voice she knew must be hers crying out for light.

It came instantly, a great slab of it almost immediately above her. And another. And another. Moon and starlight but curiously distanced, curiously artificial.

Then she knew where she was. Hut No. 7, the best preserved of all, and roofed with glass to prevent further deterioration through the weather. At night it seemed the glass roof was boarded over, to protect it from sheep perhaps, or other creatures of the dark.

Up there now was a creature of the dark, dragging aside the boards.

Caroline realised she was sitting before the central hearth. To her right and left were beds—small enclosures created by three vertical slabs. A grave had been found beneath one of these she recalled. And it was from this very hut that the woman with the broken necklace had fled.

A stronger light than moon and stars fell through the glass and sought her out. She made no attempt to evade it and peered up through the translucent screen at the figure beyond.

It was Chuff, of course. She could scarcely make out his face but imagined he looked very angry. Certainly there was something almost insanely purposeful about the way he was pointing his gun. Sandy's command about firing, his superior's directive, about her well-being—she was sure neither meant anything to this man. He advanced along the edge of the still-unremoved boards till he loomed directly overhead, blotting out the moon.

Hazlitt hadn't returned, she thought suddenly. She hoped it meant he was safe, but feared it must mean quite something else. In which case, there was not so much to fear about this man who was going to kill her.

She closed her eyes. Heard a double or treble gunshot. And a crashing of glass.

And heard nothing more.

Hazlitt had heard the first shot moments earlier.

'What the hell's that?' he demanded.

'The girl's still with you?' asked Campbell.

'Yes.'

'Not to worry. She'll be okay.' But he sounded very unconvincing.

'I'm going,' said Hazlitt, opening the car door. It was quite undramatic. Only a bullet would have stopped him. Campbell shrugged fatalistically and stepped out of the car also.

'I tell you, it's all under control,' he said. Hazlitt did not answer, but began to make his way from the car park, towards the distant line of whiteness which was the sea.

Suddenly a flurry of shots rattled the air, their flashes quite distinct over the ruined village.

'Caroline!' screamed Hazlitt, and set off at a gallop over the field. Several times he missed his footing and fell, but always rose instantly and with scarcely any loss of speed. Campbell was more circumspect and dropped far behind.

Now Hazlitt was approaching the mound. He saw figures moving in the dim light, two of them or perhaps three.

He reached the small boundary fence, half leapt, half crashed through it, and scrambled up the mound. At the top waiting for him was a woman.

'Caroline?' he said, knowing he was wrong even as he spoke.

'You're making it bloody hard to mock-up an accident,' said Cherry accusingly. She had her gun out and looked as if she were at the end of her tether.

He grabbed her by the ankles as he reached the top of the mound and dragged her feet from beneath her. She screamed as she hit the ground with a bone-cracking thud, but Hazlitt ignored her. He pressed on, narrowly avoiding falling into the first hut he came across.

Then in the moonlight he saw the glass dome with a great jagged fissure in it. Two steps took him to its edge and he looked down through the hole.

There below, frosted with moonlight, lay Caroline. She sprawled awkwardly across the ancient hearth. Her duffel bag had finally slipped from her shoulder, spilling its contents. Cheque book, American Express card, Diners' Club card, travellers cheques, all lay scattered over this floor where three thousand years earlier a woman had crouched over her cooking pots and heard the gale gathering its strength outside.

She looked peaceful lying there in her red anorak. Except that her anorak should not be red, should not be patched and stained with this still-spreading redness.

'Caroline,' he said. Somewhere close the guns started again, a giant finger flicked out of the night, striking him on the forehead, and he sank into a darkness as black as he himself would at that moment have chosen.

13

It was after seven o'clock in the morning and there were signs of activity in the Hamnavoe Hotel. Curious chambermaids glanced fleetingly through the open door of the room in which sat Lackie Campbell and a burly, slab-faced man whose only concession to being indoors was that he had unbuttoned his raincoat. They ignored the onlookers, concentrating on the whisky bottle between them, and made no attempt to close the door which gave them a clear view of the door opposite.

The view was momentarily blocked by the figure of the manager.

'How is he?' he asked sympathetically.

'He'll be all right.'

'Good. Poor Mr Coleridge, he does seem to be rather accident prone. Here's another of his friends come visiting.'

The two men stiffened, but relaxed as into the room stepped a very spruce and alert looking blond-haired young man.

' 'Morning, Smithson. Campbell. Found you at last. Where's the action?'

'The action,' said Smithson, pouring himself another large helping of Scotch, 'is over. You are too late for the action. Now we move on to the thinking. You are probably too late for the thinking as well.'

'Droll. While you two have been enjoying yourselves playing cops and robbers with Hazlitt, I've had a hell of a time fending off that bloody girl.'

The other two exchanged glances. The door opposite opened and a woman in nurse's outfit appeared.

'He's waking up,' she said.

'Thank you,' said Campbell. 'Would you like to go and have a bite of breakfast perhaps? We'll keep an eye on him.'

'Fine,' she said. 'And I'd like a wash and change o' clothes too.'

'Take your time.'

Smithson and Campbell entered the room, the fair-haired man just behind them. He stopped short when he saw the figure in bed, half risen on one elbow. It was Hazlitt, his head swathed in a huge bandage.

'My God! What happened to him?'

'A bullet clipped him,' said Campbell. 'How do you feel, Mr Hazlitt?'

'Rotten,' was the groaned reply. 'Where am I?'

'The Hamnavoe Hotel.'

'The Hamnavoe . . . ?' Hazlitt stopped short. The mists cleared and last night leapt up at him like a stand-up picture in a children's book.

'Caroline!' he said wildly. 'Where's Caroline?'

Smithson and Campbell exchanged looks once more.

'I'm sorry,' said Campbell gently. 'There was nothing we could do.'

'What? What do you mean?'

'She's dead, Mr Hazlitt,' said Smithson brusquely. 'The man, Chuff. We got him, but it was too late.'

'Oh Jesus!' It was the fair-haired man who spoke. He collapsed heavily on to a chair and shook his head in disbelief.

'Dead?' said Hazlitt. 'Oh, the bastards! The bastards!'

He sank back in the bed, turned his face to the pillow and wept.

'Yes, Mr Hazlitt,' said Smithson. 'The bastards. You've been protecting these people . . .'

Campbell stopped him, shaking his head warningly.

'Later,' he said. 'Later.'

They moved to the door, the fair-haired man following. Campbell turned to him and spoke lowly.

'Stay on here, will you, Durban? Keep an eye on him till the nurse gets back. We need a bit of rest ourselves.'

Durban nodded and returned to his seat.

Back in their own room the other two finished their drinks.

'No quotations?' enquired Smithson dryly.

'Burns knew nothing of this kind of vileness,' said Campbell.

'You Scots are all sentimentalists at heart,' said the other. 'Give him an hour, shall we? He'll be ready to tell us everything.'

He turned and threw himself full length on one of the two beds in the room. Campbell looked down at him, shrugged, closed the door and lay down on the other bed. Soon they were both asleep.

The siren of the departing ferry woke Campbell some time later and he lay on the bed staring up at the ceiling for half an hour or more.

There was a gentle tapping at the door. Quickly he rose and opened it. Outside stood the nurse.

'I'm sorry I was so long,' she said.

'That's all right. There's a friend with him.'

'Is there?' she answered, looking relieved. 'The thing is, I've tried the door and can't get in. And no one comes when I knock.'

Campbell was across the corridor in two strides. He banged hard on the door.

'Durban!' he said. 'Durban! Are you there?'

Further down the corridor a chambermaid appeared carrying bed linen. Campbell approached her smiling. Even more than royalty, men in his job were trained not to panic in public. When he returned with her master key, Smithson appeared blearily at the other door.

'What's up?' he asked.

'Nothing,' said Campbell, turning the key. Carefully he opened the door and peered in, then turned round, chuckling.

'Both fast asleep,' he said, returning the key. 'That'll be all right, Nurse. Had your breakfast yet?'

'Yes,' said the nurse.

'Fine. Then why not run along and try a coffee?'

Reluctantly the nurse left with one or two backward glances.

'What's going on?' said Smithson, fully awake now.

Campbell opened the door again and drew him inside.

On the bed, stripped to his underpants and bound and gagged with lengths of curtain cord, lay Durban.

'You bloody half-wit!' cursed Smithson.

'What happened?' demanded Campbell.

'I thought he was supposed to be ill!' answered Durban between great gasps of air. 'I'm nearly choked! The sod took my clothes. What made him do it?'

'And your gun?'

Durban looked around.

'Yes. He must have done. But he can't hope to get far, surely.'

'Only to Lincoln. The ferry! He must be on the ferry!'

'That makes it easy. That bluebottle, what's his name, Servis. He's still in Thurso, isn't he? Nice discreet kind of fellow. We'll ring him and ask him to meet the boat.'

Campbell nodded, but looked unconvinced.

'He'll have to be sharp. Hazlitt's learnt a lot very quickly. But we've got to get him!'

'Why?' asked Durban. 'What's all the fuss?'

'We just wanted names from him,' said Campbell grimly. 'But he's not giving us names. He's gone to sort out his ex-masters for himself!'

It did not take long to confirm that Hazlitt had been seen on the pier shortly before the ferry left and a phone call to Thurso alerted Servis, who spent the next hour grimly pacing up and down on the pier at Scrabster, determined that he was not going to be made a fool of again.

Two hours later, as the last car off the ferry pulled away and the two constables who had been searching the ship reappeared shaking their heads, he began to have an uneasy feeling that it had happened once more. But just in case Hazlitt were still aboard, waiting for a chance to slip ashore, Servis stood opposite the ship till, shortly after midday, it headed back to the islands.

He watched it sink beneath the horizon and said, 'Well, if he's on it, they can bloody well find him for themselves!'

But by this time Hazlitt's plane had already landed in Edinburgh and he was boarding a south-bound train.

Campbell was right. Hazlitt had learned a lot. The dangers of the ferry had been very apparent to him, so after making himself very prominent on the pier, he had slipped back into the town and caught the bus to Kirkwall. A plane had been ready to leave on his arrival at the airport. But it was completely booked up. It was, after all, the holiday season. Only a cancellation could help . . .

Hazlitt had not even had to think. Something inexorable was in control of him, something almost as tangible as the heavy automatic resting inside his waistband on his right hip.

He had looked around the small departure lounge. A

171

man had just come in with his family. His wife had a small airline bag in which clearly he kept the family's tickets and spare cash. The children ran around playing. One came near Hazlitt, his foot snaked out, the girl tripped, fell and began to cry noisily over her cut knee. Mother came to the rescue. When she had finished first-aid, her bag had gone.

Hazlitt left it on the cistern in the Gents' a few minutes before departure time and approached the desk. Yes, there had been a cancellation. Four, in fact. He was lucky.

As the plane lifted from the runway, he hoped someone honest would find the bag. But it didn't bother him much.

Curiously there was no element of impatience in this terrible concentration of feeling. The train snaked south through the Border Country, on to Newcastle, Darlington, York, and he felt no resentment of its stops, its delays. At York he got out. No plan. He just knew this was the right thing to do. Lincoln station would be watched, and perhaps the main-line stations at one of which he would normally expect to change—Doncaster, Retford, Newark.

He hired a car. The deposit took nearly all that remained of Caroline's money. Fortunately there was a driving licence among the other things in the suit he had stolen from Durban. His old antipathy to cars seemed to have disappeared, just as his old absorption with food and drink had done. He had eaten nothing since he and Caroline had sat by the sea near Skara Brae, sharing a pork pie and some apples.

He found he could recall the scene without emotion. It was like thinking about some completely different person. He smiled to himself, pleased with the change. For he knew that that completely different person who had sat by the girl, and made love to her, and woken with her head on his chest, could not have taken a gun and walked into a room and shot a man between the eyes as he rose with a friendly smile to meet him.

And this was precisely what the new person he now found himself to be intended doing.

A sign loomed up telling him he was nearing Doncaster. Good, good, he thought. Another couple of hours and it would be all over. He pressed harder on the accelerator and started overtaking a long string of lorries. In the distance he could see a car approaching, but it was too far away to present any threat and the last of the lorry-drivers was cheerfully waving him by.

Then, as though by use of trick photography, the approaching car seemed to double in size, its headlights blazed, its horn trumpeted, the lorry-driver's arm was waving him back and the grim face which peered down at him from the cab's height was mouthing fearful abuse.

The oncoming car braked, the lorry braked, and the combination was just sufficient to permit him to squeeze back to his own side of the road.

He pulled up at the next lay-by and sat in complete passivity for a quarter of an hour.

Hate was not enough, he decided. It gave you impetus, but did not prevent gross errors of judgment. What he was going to do would offer no second chances.

I am hungry, he told himself. I am tired. I am hurt. My hunger needs food, my fatigue rest and my sickness medicine. These are needs which clearly refuse to wait, whereas the need of my hatred which is revenge cannot harm me by waiting a little.

He thought this put the case rather elegantly and was pleased to find he still had such powers of logical self-control.

In Doncaster he had a large meal, booked a room at an hotel, changed the dressing on his head wound, took four aspirins and went to bed.

173

The darkness which came when he turned off the light was primal. The usual gradual emergence of shapes and outlines did not take place and the darkness remained unchallenged until the early hours of the morning when his mind was split by the flash of gunfire and he woke up weeping that Caroline was dead.

'This has been a balls-up from start to finish.'

Campbell and Smithson said nothing, but Durban, who had arrived late, thought to ingratiate himself by nodding vigorous agreement. All he succeeded in doing was to concentrate on himself the full disapproval of the Old Etonian.

'Gun battles, people dying, my agents losing their guns and trousers, and now I have to be in Lincoln during Goodwood.'

He made this last sound like the most disastrous consequence of their inefficiency.

'And while we're sitting here this man Hazlitt is wandering around loose, planning to murder somebody.'

Smithson spoke.

'It's all right, sir. We've taken precautions . . .'

'Precautions! Like the precautions you took when you had him in Stromness? Understand me, I don't want anyone killed here in Lincoln, not even if he turns out to be the head of the KGB himself. Orkney's one thing, Lincolnshire is quite another.'

Again Smithson spoke, soothingly, reassuringly.

'It's all under control, sir. We've got the situation well covered . . .'

Again he was interrupted.

'Covered!' exclaimed the Old Etonian, flinging up his slim pale hands in exaggerated despair. 'How can you cover what you don't know? Who is it that this maniac is going to try to kill? You've no idea, have you? And one thing is certain in this business. It's probably the last person on earth you would suspect. Have you any idea at all?'

Durban nodded vigorously in agreement, then changed the movement to an equally vigorous shake. The other two looked glumly at the floor.

A few miles away Professor James Nevis was looking uneasily at the tall bald-headed man who sat opposite him. The weariness of a long journey had deepened the lines in his face, but did not obscure the power and authority of the features.

'I don't feel you've conducted this business well,' said the man, his dark grey eyes fixed accusingly on the professor.

'I'm sorry,' said Nevis. 'But what else could I have done? I've suffered a great deal too.'

'You undertook responsibility. I believed you could be trusted,' said the bald man. 'Now I have to come. You know I do not care to be here.'

'Really,' said Nevis in protest, 'I hardly think you can blame me. It was none of my idea to start with, you recall. The way people turn out is the responsibility of those who have control of them at the formative stage and I don't . . .'

'Enough,' interrupted the man. 'I'm too tired to argue. You say you have no idea where Hazlitt is?'

'None.'

'He must be found. I must talk to him. Then we will decide what to do. But it must be quickly, you understand that. Once I am missed at home, questions will be asked, then hell will be let loose for us all. There'll be no question of allotting responsibility. You understand?'

'Yes, I understand,' said Nevis glumly, staring into his empty glass. He had known it would work out badly. Poor Caroline . . . He reached for the whisky decanter.

14

At ten o'clock in the morning of the second day after his flight from Orkney, Hazlitt returned to Lincoln. It was less than three weeks since he had left, thinking that something could be solved by hiding himself for a while in the mountains of Skye. He had been foolish then, naive to the point of stupidity. How much more mature and rational his behaviour was now.

The automatic fitted snugly into the jacket pocket which he had carefully enlarged the previous day. He had practised a rapid draw for a while, but decided in the end that he was no Billy the Kid and if necessary to fire through the pocket at close range would be just as efficient and accurate. Another mature and rational decision.

The bandage round his head had been replaced by a piece of plaster covering the bullet graze on his brow. He had shaved off the garden-gnome beard which had grown during his days in the wilds. And using Durban's cheque book he had purchased himself a new and rather better-fitting set of clothes.

Now as he looked at himself in the mirror of the telephone box in which he stood, he saw a fair replica of his old persona. A little thinner round the cheeks perhaps. And a genuine wind-and-sun-daubed tan had replaced the old near-vinous flush. But recognisably and unremarkably Willian Blake Hazlitt, Deputy Registrar, a man with a fine future behind him.

He heard the answering tone at the other end of the line and pressed in his money.

A voice he did not recognise answered and for a moment he was disconcerted.

'I was just ringing to find if Professor Nevis were at home,' he said finally.

'No,' replied the voice. 'He's at a meeting at the university. Who's speaking, please?'

'It doesn't matter,' said Hazlitt. 'Thank you.'

'Who is that?' said the voice, suddenly becoming urgent. 'Hello! Hello!'

Hazlitt replaced the receiver and stood in thought for a while. He should have remembered. Wednesday. Nevis would be going to the monthly meeting of the Establishment Committee. That complicated matters. But he must move swiftly now. It had been a mistake ringing Nevis's house. Whoever it was who answered had sounded faintly suspicious.

He returned to his car and drove swiftly to the university. The car-park attendant came striding officiously across the tarmac at the sight of this strange car being parked into an official spot, but rearranged his features into an ingratiating smile when he recognised Hazlitt.

Hazlitt did not return it, but strode purposefully into the main admin block, the ground floor of which comprised the registry.

A door opened as he moved down the main corridor.

'Well, Billy! Welcome back!'

It was Tarquin Adam, looking very smooth in puce mohair.

'Hello, Tarquin,' said Hazlitt. Something was missing, he thought. Suddenly he realised what it was. Somehow Tarquin had always intimidated him. Background, manner, clothes, all these combined with the good looks of a young Greek god had made him a powerful symbol of what Hazlitt wasn't. Now it didn't matter. There was nothing there any more. A small thing, but it gave Hazlitt his first distant echo of pleasure for forty-eight hours.

'Didn't expect you back so soon,' said Tarquin ironically. 'Stuart will be delighted to see you.'

'Yes,' said Hazlitt, preparing to move on.

'Shouldn't disturb him now, though. Old "Ben" Nevis is in there, with him. They're preparing some kind of little bomb for the Establishment Committee.'

'The meeting hasn't started?'

'Oh no. Another fifteen minutes to go. Sholto's with them, keeping your end up, so you needn't worry.'

'I won't,' said Hazlitt.

He went down the corridor till he reached his own office which he entered. Inside, another door led to the room shared by his own and the Registrar's secretary. And from this room yet another door led into the Registrar's own office.

The secretary's room was empty, he was pleased to find. Miss Plackett's coy delight at his return was more than he could have faced just now.

He listened at Stuart's door for a while, then went back to his own room and picked up the phone.

He dialled and heard the phone ring on Stuart's desk.

'Yes?' It was Sholto's voice. He could envisage the imperious gesture with which Stuart had commanded him to answer it.

Hazlitt deepened and thickened his own voice.

'Porter's office here, sir. Is Professor Nevis with you by any chance?'

'Yes, he is.'

'Well, sir, there's a policeman here would like a word with him. Urgent, he says. Inspector Servis is the name.'

'Hold on.'

A pause. That should bring him. It was useful remembering the name of Caroline's policeman like that. But the concomitant memory of Caroline drew a line of pain through his head.

'Hello, Professor Nevis is on his way.'

Hazlitt replaced the phone, drew his automatic, and shifted the safety catch to 'off'.

In the next room he heard a door open and close. Quickly he stepped up to the communicating door which he had left ajar.

Through it he saw Nevis. He seemed to have aged considerably since last they met and Hazlitt felt a pang of genuine pity for the man.

He hefted the gun in his hand. The moment had almost come.

Then something hard dug deep into the base of his spine and behind him a quiet voice said, 'Thank you, sir. I think I'll have that.'

Hazlitt turned. Behind him stood Smithson, whom he recognised as Tom (Mark I), the man in the boat visiting Coruisk.

'So I was right about you,' he said.

'Very likely, sir. Now the gun.'

But Hazlitt held on to it. In the next room, attracted by their voices, Nevis had paused at the outer door. Now he turned and stared in amazement.

'Hazlitt,' he said. 'My God!'

But he said no more. The outer door opened and Campbell and Durban appeared, seized his arms and like an expertly drilled music-hall chorus the three of them moved backwards into the corridor and the door closed behind, or, rather, in front of them.

'There now, sir. That's that little matter out of the way. Now the gun.'

But Hazlitt, after a moment of utter incomprehension, was laughing.

'You don't think . . . Oh God! No wonder we're . . .'

Puzzled by the laughter, Smithson relaxed. Hazlitt's gun hand came scything round, the heavy automatic caught Smithson on the point of the elbow and he shrieked in agony, dropping his own gun to the floor.

Hazlitt turned and flung himself across the room, bursting through Stewart Stuart's door with a violence that stunned the occupants.

The Registrar recovered first and slowly began to rise, staring fixedly at the gun.

'Hazlitt,' he said. 'For God's sake, I had nothing to do with them trying to kill you. Believe me. I knew you'd say nothing. It was this fool here. Sholto, tell him . . . !'

But Sholto was too busy with his own thoughts to pay any heed.

'I protected you,' said Hazlitt. 'I regarded you as a friend and I protected you. But still your thugs came after me. But it's not that, oh no, that's not the reason I'm going to kill you. You know that, don't you?'

'What then?' cried Stuart.

'The girl. Caroline.'

'Nevis's daughter? But why . . . ?'

Sholto launched himself over the desk, caught his knee on the edge and fell well short. Hazlitt raised his gun. Behind him he was conscious that Smithson had recovered. In fact he seemed to be standing close by his side but was making no attempt to interfere.

He aimed down at Sholto and pressed the trigger twice. Before the echoes of these blasts had even begun to die, the gun was pointing at Stuart's paunch and spitting flames again. And again. And again.

Till finally the convulsive pressure of his finger on the trigger produced only a harmless click.

Slowly Hazlitt lowered the weapon and looked at what he had done.

He had only seen three corpses in his life. The first had been his mother's, peacefully lying in her coffin; the second had been Tom (Mark II)'s, bloody but decently arranged in a funeral-parlour parody; the last had been Caroline's.

The two men before him resembled none of these.

There was no blood. They did not lie still. Their faces had assumed no fixity of expression.

In fact they stood, and moved, and seemed completely uninjured. And on their faces the emotion of sheer black terror was gradually turning to one of incredulous relief.

'Well, I hope you enjoyed that, sir,' said Smithson kindly. 'Gentlemen, please take your seats and try to smile. I'm afraid we may have attracted a little attention.'

The outer door burst open and Durban appeared in the secretary's room, waving a gun.

'What's happened?' he exclaimed. 'We heard . . .'

'Put that thing away!' snapped Smithson. 'Quick!'

Durban managed it just before Tarquin appeared at the door.

'I say,' he said. 'What's all the row? It sounded like . . .'

But his voice faded away under the uninformative stares of all those present.

'It's all right,' said Stuart suddenly. 'Just a little joke. New method of settling disputes on the Establishment Committee.'

He managed a small laugh. Smithson took it up, and Durban.

Puzzled, Tarquin withdrew.

'I liked that,' said Smithson approvingly to Stuart. 'Still hoping to survive. Good. Durban, run along and tell Campbell to release Professor Nevis with some story or other. I take it we've made a mistake about Professor Nevis, sir?'

'Oh yes. You've made a mistake,' said Hazlitt.

'I thought so. Quick as you like, Durban.'

'Are we under arrest?' said Sholto mildly. The relief at still being alive had not yet evaporated.

'Nothing like that, sir. Not yet.'

The outer door opened again and Nevis entered, talking to Campbell.

'No,' he said. 'I will not go away quietly and give a lecture. I demand to know what the hell's going on. Hazlitt, what the hell's happening, man? Who are these people? You've got a great deal of explaining to do.'

'Yes,' said Hazlitt dully. A terrible feeling of anticlimax had come upon him. He had come through all this for nothing. Not even the cloudy trophies of accomplished vengeance were his to contemplate in the emptiness of his life.

'I tried to get in touch before,' he said. 'Before I this . . .'

He gestured towards Stuart and Sholto, realising he made no sense.

'I just wanted to say . . . how sorry I was . . . Caroline . . .'

He could say no more. Nevis looked puzzled, Campbell and Smithson embarrassed.

'About Caroline? I should think you need to explain quite a lot there. But not to me, thank God, though you'll probably wish . . .'

He broke off and turned away to look into the corridor.

'Ah,' he said. 'Caroline.'

For a second Hazlitt thought he had broken down and had turned away like a British gentleman to hide his grief.

Then a girl appeared in the doorway.

'What the hell do you mean by stealing all my money and running off?' she demanded.

Behind her stood a tall bald-headed man, sombrefaced and regarding Hazlitt with grave distrust. Hazlitt had never seen him before.

183

'Bill, darling,' said the girl. 'I'd like you to meet my father. And you might look a little more overjoyed to see me.'

'Caroline,' said Hazlitt. All at once he knew how it felt to be one of those characters who find at the end of a Shakesperian play that someone thought to be dead is alive. But they had Shakespeare to write their lines for them, whereas all he could say, his eyes fixed on Caroline as though a blink would make her disappear, was, 'I'd like a drink.'

15

'You really have been a naughty boy, Mr Hazlitt,' said the Old Etonian reprovingly. 'Having said that, I must admit that the behaviour of my own men has left a great deal to be desired. What can I say or do to atone?'

'You can start by changing your wine merchant,' said Hazlitt, sniffing at the glass of sherry which he had just been given.

'Is it not good?' asked the Old Etonian anxiously.

'They make this stuff in Cyprus by urinating on raisins,' said Hazlitt. He felt little urge to accept this man's conciliatory gestures. He very much doubted their sincerity and was doubly annoyed to find his palate being affronted as well as his intelligence.

'And drop the apologetic manner,' he went on. 'You got what you wanted. So you can stuff your phony regrets.'

For answer the Old Etonian went over to the telephone and dialled room service.

'A bottle of Remy Martin,' he said.

Hazlitt nodded approvingly.

'You're right, of course,' said the Old Etonian. 'But they didn't act on orders, believe me. Our notion was that if we followed you around long enough, you'd either make contact with your man, or you'd get sick of being chased by those three comic-opera thugs and give us his name of your own volition.'

'I doubt it.'

'Yes. You're an oddly loyal person, Mr Hazlitt. So when you got creased by dear Cherry's last bullet and it became apparent through your delirious babblings that you feared Miss Nevis were dead, it seemed too good an opportunity to miss. As I'm sure the lady has told you, what happened was that our Mr Smithson, who had gone from the car park to collect Miss Nevis, discovered the man, Chuff, trying to kill her. He shot him and down he fell through the glass roof right on top of her, knocking her unconscious. He then bled copiously all over her before dragging himself off into the passageway where I regret to say he did not die.'

'Pity,' said Hazlitt.

The bottle of cognac arrived and they started drinking.

'But all my men planned to do,' resumed the Old Etonian, 'was to use your mistaken belief that Miss Nevis was dead to get the names from you. An hour or so's tragic sorrow followed almost immediately by joyful reunion. Instead you decided to do your own dirty work. Surprising. And uncharacteristic.'

'Uncharacteristic?'

'Yes. After the horror you expressed at the prospect of helping Colonel Oto shuffle off this mortal coil . . . but circumstances alter cases, I suppose.'

'May I help myself?' asked Hazlitt, seizing the brandy bottle.

'Please do. You're very good at it, it seems.'

'Thanks. All this doesn't explain how the gun I took from one of your agents was loaded with blanks. Or don't you trust that one with live ammunition?'

'Poor Durban,' said the Old Etonian. 'I sometimes think we shouldn't. No, I'm afraid you left a rather wide trail down from Scotland. It took a little time for us to get on it, but after that it was easy. The blank clip was substituted in your hotel bedroom. And a small bugging device fitted so that we could keep track of you. Even then your concern with Professor Nevis disconcerted us rather.'

'I just wanted to talk to him about Caroline,' said Hazlitt. 'Then when I found he was in the room with those other two I wanted to get him out of the way.'

'Considerate,' said the Old Etonian approvingly. 'Let me replenish your glass. Now, other matters. No one proposes to proceed with any charges against you. At the moment.'

'That sounds like a threat,' said Hazlitt.

'I'm sorry. It is a threat, of course, but it wasn't meant to sound like one. No, I was just wondering about your future.'

'My future?'

'Yes. Stewart Stuart is resigning, of course. And I'm assured the post is yours for the asking. But I wondered if you might now be more receptive to an offer of alternative, or perhaps simply additional, employment?'

'Like poisoning Oto? No thanks!'

'No, no. Things have changed. Oto is approved of in Westminster now, don't you read your papers? We are *protecting* Oto.'

'That's nice. Look, about Stuart, what happens to him?'

'Oh, he'll be all right, never fear. They always are. They have a choice, you know. Full co-operation and stop here in comfort. Or go to jail, move directly to jail, and hope for a quick exchange.'

'And which has he opted for?'

'Who knows? Perhaps you'd like a word with him. Might help you make up your mind about my offer.'

'Why are you so keen to recruit me?' asked Hazlitt, genuinely puzzled.

'You have the right qualifications, Mr Hazlitt. Over

these past two or three weeks you've proved you're a man of fortitude, courage, ingenuity; physically fit, mentally alert, great powers of survival.'

Hazlitt preened himself, flattered in spite of anything he could do to resist.

'But your main attraction,' added the Old Etonian, 'is that to look at you, all this would appear completely out of the question, I mean, just impossible, wouldn't you agree?'

'Hello, Bill,' said Stuart.

'How are they treating you?'

'Oh, I'm very comfortable. Very.'

'What will you do?'

'Don't think too badly of me, but I'm going to co-operate. Yes. Co-operate.'

'Co-operate?'

'That's it. I'm sixty-five. I don't want to go to prison. I don't particularly want to go to Moscow and live on a pension, even if they'd bother to exchange me. So it's the only way.'

'I'm sorry, Stewart. I'm sorry I ever found out about you.'

'Yes. Well, I was getting old. Careless. I'd done my party service in Whitehall. Lincoln was honourable retirement for me. And in any case I knew you were to be trusted. Not as a party member, perhaps, but as a friend. I was right, wasn't I?'

'Yes. I'm sorry I tried to . . .'

'Not your fault. Not your fault. I told that fool Sholto not to set his thugs on you.'

'I knew that couldn't be you. In fact, I'd made up my mind to come back and talk to you when, well, when I thought Caroline got killed. Then it all changed. You seemed to merit some of the blame then. What'll happen to Sholto?'

188

Stuart began to laugh.

'He's keeping a tight mouth, it seems. Imagines he'll be exchanged pretty quick. But once they realise I've co-operated, nothing he knows is worth getting him out for. Not by either side.'

'Poor Sholto. It's a dirty business.'

'Most of what makes life fascinating is, don't you think? Be careful. It can grip you unawares. May I come and see you when I'm out and about again?'

'I insist on it. We'll always welcome you.'

'We?'

'Yes. I'm thinking of getting married.'

'Bill, I'd like you to meet my mother.'

'Hello, Bill! He looks fine to me, honey, just fine. When I found out that John was over here and not at the conference in Chicago like he said he was, well I went wild, I was so sure something dreadful must have happened, you know, I mean something dreadful!'

'Such as, Mrs Nevis?'

'Well, you know how young people are these days, so when I heard your name mentioned I naturally imagined some long-haired way-out yippie had got my baby into trouble, you know, with drugs or politics, or sex, that kind of thing, but now I've met you, Bill, I can see at once how wrong I was to worry about any of those things. You don't know how much of a relief it is to see you in the flesh, Bill, and have my fears set at rest.'

'I suppose your husband has mentioned to you that Caroline and I hope to get married, Mrs Nevis.'

'Married! My little baby married?'

'I'm twenty-five, Mother.'

'I know that, dear. I was a young bride myself, Mr Hazlitt. Well, *married*! This is going to take a deal of arranging when we get back, John. A deal of arranging.'

She looked at her husband, her mind full of gowns

189

and flowers and ministers and presents and catering and friends and relations, while her husband stared glumly at Hazlitt and thought of the young, clean-cut third- or fourth-generation American boy with a great career in plastics before him that he had desired for his daughter. James Nevis looked on with a polite smile, hoping that perhaps this news would get his garrulous sister-in-law and holier-than-thou brother back to America with great expedition, looking forward to his niece's departure from his house, and planning to have the swimming pool filled in immediately.

Hazlitt and Caroline looked at each other, thinking quite unthinkable things.

Mrs Nevis returned to them.

'Just think, honey. Mrs Hazlitt! That's a fine-sounding name. Wasn't there some famous old English writer with that name, Mr Hazlitt?'

'There was indeed,' said Hazlitt. 'He was a journalist of revolutionary principles, who took drugs, had an unhappy marriage and abandoned his wife to go in pursuit of a servant girl who despised him. I think I'm distantly related.'

'That was pretty cruel to my mother, that thing about Hazlitt,' said Caroline reprovingly.

'English humour,' said Hazlitt. 'She must get used to it.'

'You're condescending again,' said Caroline warningly.

'Sorry.'

They were walking by the swimming pool in Professor Nevis's garden. It was a glorious evening, and in the west the death of day was being directed with all the fine disregard for taste and restraint of the best Hollywood musicals.

'Anyway, my mother had you pegged at first sight,'

mocked Caroline. 'She was scared I was being ravished thrice nightly and perhaps in the lunch hour too, but the minute she saw you, she knew I was safe.'

'It's a good job she wasn't around at Skara Brae,' said Hazlitt smugly. 'I heard no complaints then.'

'No. You're right, though a gentleman wouldn't have reminded me. Yeah, I guess appearances can be deceptive.'

'That seems to be the thought for the day,' said Hazlitt, thinking of the Old Etonian. Caroline seemed to catch the edge of the thought and looked at him anxiously.

'It is all over, isn't it, Bill? All this secret-agent business, I mean.'

'Of course,' he said, crossing his fingers behind his back.

'It's all so creepy. You never know who's doing what. Poor Stewart Stuart. You're getting his job?'

'If I want it.'

'What do you want, Bill?' she asked seriously.

He smiled affectionately at her. She was really a very serious person. That's what had kept her going during her crazy chase all over Scotland. But you could be too serious.

'Well,' he answered. 'It was Lackie Campbell who put me on to it.'

Striking a pose and adopting an abominable Scots accent, he recited :

> 'Fortune! if thou'll but gie me still
> Hale breeks, a scone, an' whiskey gill,
> An' rowth o' rhyme to rave at will,
>   Tak' a' the rest,
> An' deal't about as thy blind skill
>   Directs thee best!'

'Those are pretty simple needs,' said Caroline.

'I'm a pretty simple fellow.'

In the west now the sky and horizon were flat, a simple wash of dark blue broken by lines of chimneys and trees in unshaded black. The vulgarities of the Hollywood musical sunset had gone and the cartoonist had taken over from the cameraman. It was a Tom and Jerry evening. And the cat and the mouse, Hazlitt now recognised, were really the same, interchangeable, complementary. And even though he now knew from experience that when Tom fell and shattered into a thousand pieces or Jerry had his head twisted round till his neck was like a corkscrew, they did not miraculously regain their shape and wholeness and resume pursuit and flight, he also knew that this mattered surprisingly little.

It's a dirty business, Stuart had said, but it can grip you unawares.

'Penny for your thoughts,' said Caroline.

'Back at my flat,' said Hazlitt, 'I have a bottle of Montrachet which I don't care to leave undrunk any longer.'

'Lead me to it,' said Caroline.

They went up the garden path together. In the west the cartoonist's brush at last washed the far horizon out of sight and with little stabbing strokes began to open up the eyes of the stars.